Please Read Before Dying

Jonathan Moon

Copyright © 2023 Jonathan Moon

All rights reserved.

ISBN: 979-8-3906-82807

For Ms. Mole, thank you for putting the pen back in my hand.

CONTENTS

One	1
Two	13
Three	22
Four	32
Five	40
Six	46
Seven	61
Eight	73
Nine	87
Ten	96
Eleven	105
Twelve	119
Thirteen	130
Fourteen	136
Fifteen	150
Sixteen	162
Seventeen	173
Eighteen	187
Nineteen	194
Twenty	203
Twenty-one	212

ONE

Grey fidgeted in an office chair, unaware he would be dead in seven hours. Of course, very few are ever aware of their impending death.

Although he was a chronic fidgeter, these particular fidgets were the kind that he only performed when feeling particularly frustrated at work, for example, when a dry and dragging meeting like this one could have easily been an email. It was late afternoon and the shadows from the pearly blinds stretched across the conference room table, and time seemed to slow to within an inch of Grey questioning whether someone was messing around with the cosmic playback rate.

His colleagues droned on about less than nothing, whilst Grey nodded at the appropriate moments and checked his watch, which seemed to drum in moments like this, eager to report the end of the hour.

There was another meeting, a far more interesting and important meeting, begging for Grey's attention. One that didn't seek to suck out his energy through bureaucracy and office politics, and it was a mere hour away. Grey's financial advisor, (and dare he think it, friend?) had called him in to discuss a creative solution for a challenge that Grey had lost sleep over.

He wanted to find a way to keep control of his finances after death. Unfortunately, pesky laws had started popping up to stop this. Only a decade earlier, The Perpetuities and Accumulations Act of 2009 had set out, for the first time, what rights you had to your wealth post-mortem: not many. You could trust your beloved relatives to keep hold of it for you (fat chance), or you could perhaps invest it in some you-worshipping cult that would wait for your second coming. The Act was designed to stop people from taking assets out of the economy when they died, like the pharaohs who buried themselves with vast wealth (and subsequently almost always had their tombs raided). And for Grey, tomb-raiding was a very modern issue, as he had planned for reanimation after death in very certain terms (after, of course, a long and prosperous life).

Grey's attention was momentarily needed again in his meeting and he confirmed that his plan for the next quarter was drafted and readily available on the shared drive, before shifting his gaze to Cat's scalp. Her roots were coming in. Little sprouts of silver were blooming faster than she could colour them with her usual coppery-golden hair dye. Grey gritted his teeth a little. Life was about presentation and planning, after all. His dad had carefully hammered that point into him from childhood.

To his right, Matthew clicked his clicky pen against his front teeth. The notepad in front of him was splattered with ink smears and smudges, which no doubt could be found reflected on the edge of his palms. He had this daft habit of brushing his hand across his page every time he scrawled down a note, as if in the millisecond that his pen had left the paper, a layer of dust had settled which needed to be dealt with.

Handwriting: Messy.

Grey noted that Matthew had misspelt 'account' and it took everything to stop himself rolling his eyes.

Spelling: Atrocious.

"In a market this volatile..." James said, in that nasty nasally voice of his, stretching the word to an impossible four syllables. 'Vol-uh-ty-el'. Unnecessary syllables for an unnecessary meeting.

Next to James was possibly the only person in the room more useless than Matthew. Charlie was a recent graduate whose uncle was a close personal friend of the 'Lyle' half of Smith and Lyle Marketing. Charlie often arrived at meetings late, unprepared, swaggering in with that stupid uneven grin and performative insistence that everybody call him 'Chaz'. Grey would sooner call him 'unemployed'.

Grey didn't think he could bear it for much longer. His other, more titillating meeting was getting closer. The office was across town, he could make it in twenty minutes, but with traffic- he might have to change his plan and take the train. He shook his head slightly to clear some of the tightness in his chest. There was very little he hated more than being late. Being late spoke to an inability to manage one's schedule. It hinted at life being overwhelming, at a breakdown in the system somehow. An inability to plan ahead, a detail missed, a wrench in the day.

Finally, blessedly, the meeting ended. Matthew wiped his page one, twice, thrice more, promising to make photocopies for the rest of the team while Cat scuttled off to what Grey hoped was a much-needed salon appointment. Grey gathered his things calmly, efficiently. Tucking his pen and notes into his bag with practiced hands. Nobody observing would ever suspect him of being in a hurry, let alone agitated. He was the picture of control in all things, even as he chose to forgo the elevator in favour of the stairs, which he raced down two at a time. Outside, he hailed a black taxi and climbed in, heart thumping in anticipation of eternal life, and more importantly, riches.

*

The lobby of Piety Financial was dressed in slabs of quartz and granite polished to a glassy shine, giving the impression it had been carved entirely out of stone. Grey pushed his way through the glass doors and made his way to reception, his shoes eliciting tiny squeaky sounds out of the floor. He smiled comfortably at the secretary, enjoying the way her cheeks ever so slightly coloured as he approached. He imagined she must find him intimidating, in his perfect suit. His very presence there would confirm that he had money, of course. Working the desk at a place like this meant that she encountered extraordinary wealth on a daily basis, but how many of these wealthy men were young enough to be eligible?

"Grey for Jeffrey Williams at 4:30," he said, checking his watch one more time. 4:26. He smiled. Wrench avoided. He allowed himself a slow, indulgent smile at the receptionist, accepting her returning smile as a reward for his timeliness.

"Of course, Sir," said the secretary. "One moment." Her voice was deeper and softer than he imagined. Like honey and cloves. She tapped on her earpiece and said, "Jeff, I have your 4:30."
She typed something into her computer with long, delicate fingers, and pursed her glossy lips.

"Who let this guy in the building?" called a joking voice.

"You're late," Grey answered the man as he emerged from his office.

"Good to see you too, Grey. You look tired." Jeff had a solid, calming sort of air about him. He was the sort of person who seemed to be as comfortable in the boardroom as he was in the pub. He was handsome, but not intimidatingly so, with salt and pepper hair and a firm handshake, which he offered to Grey. He was composed and predictable in a way that Grey had always found reassuring. An equal in every way.

"Charming as always," said Grey with a laugh.

"Up all night running the town?" Jeff asked.

"You're always welcome to join, Jeffrey,"

"Jesus, Grey. How many times do I need to ask you to call me Jeff?"

Grey returned the handshake with a smile. "What do you have for me?"

Jeff's eyes glinted with excitement. He was a brilliant financial advisor and Grey had provided him with the puzzle of the year. It looked like he just might have the solution.

"Let's go and sit down," he said, leading Grey through a door and into a private office. Jeff gestured for Grey to sit and turned to the drizzly London skyline visible through the wall of windows. It took everything in Grey not to fidget in his seat.

"Well?" he prompted.

"I've been thinking about your predicament," said Jeff. "I've got to admit, there's not a lot out there on this. Retaining wealth after death just isn't on many of my clients' minds." He turned back to Grey, taking his seat behind his desk, a beautiful, polished mahogany monstrosity that housed a sleek silver computer and a small stack of papers. It echoed the rest of the office: clean, functional, and empirically impressive with its skyline view.

"Yeah, yeah, 'No persons shall retain assets post-mortem in any account, bonds, or trust' etc. I understand the legislation. But really, is it post-mortem if I have no intention of staying dead?" asked Grey wryly. "Can we honestly consider vitrification dying in the first place?"

Jeff's lip quirked up. "I'm afraid the law doesn't account for science fiction at the moment. The economy can't handle people tucking away millions with no proposed end date. There is a chance, not insignificant I might add, that you never wake up at all."

Grey frowned. The thought had occurred to him, of course. He understood how it sounded to Jeff. Like a far-off fantasy. The last-ditch effort of a man battling his mortality, trying to live forever. Grey was a planner, always had been and always would be. And he was an excellent strategist at that. Why wouldn't he take his ability to impact the longevity of a corporation and apply it to his own life? Why wouldn't he plan his death in a way that gave him another shot? An insurance policy of sorts.

The science was there. The technology for vitrification already existed - it was more than a chance. Vitrification is a lot more sophisticated than the early Cryogenic Freezing technologies that popped up through the 90s. At the end of Grey's life - hopefully around 90, but this plan accounted for an unplanned disaster at any age - his circulation and blood pressure would be maintained whilst slowly, a replacement fluid of cryoprotectants would be injected into his body. This fluid would suffuse his cells enough to prevent the formation of ice crystals before his body is dipped in liquid nitrogen (-195C) where virtually no chemical activity can occur in the body. Then, when the technology advanced in the future, he could be re-animated and given the latest life-extending healthcare. Simple really. *If* the technology advanced.

But he didn't waste much time worrying about that. If there was one thing the human race could be counted on, it was finding ways to cheat the system.

"Assume I will wake up," said Grey.

"Right," Jeff said with a little cough. Grey noticed a hint of scepticism that he could hardly ignore.

"Listen, Jeffrey," he sighed. "I'm not here to debate my choices or the advancements of medical science. My question is this: how do I keep my money? There's hardly much reason to extend my life if I'm going to wake up poor."

Jeff smiled. "Fair point," he steepled his fingers under his chin and considered Grey for a moment. "There is no regulated institution that allows you to keep your wealth after death. Traditionally, wealth is passed on to the next of kin in lieu of a will stating otherwise, but of course that's not what we're dealing with. The way I see it, you have two choices,"

"Which are?" Grey leaned forward in his seat, heart thumping.

"Have you considered buried treasure?" Jeff asked with a chuckle. "My sister-in-law works in antiques, I can get you a great deal on a pirate's chest,"

"I'm not one for manual labour," said Grey dryly.

"Then that leaves us with the second option," said Jeff. "Are you familiar with cryptocurrencies?"

"I am," said Grey, raising a brow.

"Excellent," said Jeff. "Then what I am suggesting is this: we transfer your wealth into a cryptocurrency that's only accessible with a seed phrase. It's the best of both worlds: you can spend it now, and the law couldn't touch it in the event of your, um…Arcanum would be my recommendation - it offers the best security for something like this and has great long-term prospects. A little greener than its competitors, too. The Arcanum tokens are stored in a virtual wallet that can be accessed by anyone who knows the seed phrase or password,"

"And if nobody knows the password?" asked Grey

"It's as if the money never existed. In fact, the money *only* exists if you know the password," said Jeff.

"So, when I reanimate,"

"You simply have to access the account with the seed phrase, and it will be as if you never left," Jeff sat back in his chair with a satisfied smile.

There was a moment of stunned silence while both men considered each other.

"Genius," Grey breathed. "Jeffrey, you're a genius,"

"I am," Jeff conceded.

"Do it," said Grey, leaping to his feet and pacing the room with his excited energy. "Transfer all my discretionary funds. You know which accounts?"

"Now, hold on," said Jeff. "There are some considerations,"

"Such as?"

"You do still have a will - are you leaving anything to friends and family? Are you donating anything to charity?"

Grey snorted. "Absolutely not. Charities that pay millionaire CEOs. Always felt like a bit of a scam to me."

"Family then? Any siblings?"

Grey stilled. The tightness was back in his chest.

"No," he said softly. "Nobody that I'm close to,"

Jeff blinked impassively. Grey found it difficult to meet the man's eyes. Jeffrey was a family man. He could see Grey's lack of familial affiliation as a crack in the facade.

"All right," said Jeff, mercifully ending the silence. "Arcanum it is then,"

Grey lowered himself back into the seat with a deep breath. "Arcanum it is, and upon death all other assets in my possession can be liquidated and used to purchase more Arcanum for my account."

They spent some time going over its logistics - which accounts to move and what to keep, and Grey felt that surging energy return to him. A puzzle solved, another insurance policy in the books, a life and death finally in perfect order.

"We should celebrate," he said when they finished. "Let me buy you a drink for a job well done."

"I wish I could," said Jeff, gathering his papers and stuffing them into his briefcase. "But the missus is waiting."

"Tomorrow then? Or Thursday?" asked Grey.

Jeff winced. "The kids have football, rehearsals, and whatnot. It's a crazy week. Another time?"

"Absolutely," said Grey. "Anytime."

Jeff slid a sheet of paper across the desk to Grey. "Your instructions."

Grey picked it up, folded it in half and tucked it reverently in his pocket. "Thank you,"

*

The city buzzed below, lights winking in the darkness like fireflies as pedestrians strolled in and out of bars dizzy with alcohol and cigarettes in hand. Cars smeared the streets as they passed, belching great plumes of pollution into the ever-growing smog above them, whilst the acidic rain pelted from above, rinsing the streets clean once again.

Grey absently people watched as he stirred his Manhattan, his mind wandering away from the bright tangle of humanity to his laptop, humming softly on his coffee table.

Contrary to the excitement below, the apartment was startlingly quiet. While the street noise stirred and wafted like an odd, disjointed sort of symphony, Grey was cocooned high above with only the soft whisper of a fan. He revelled in it, like a fairy-tale prince with all the secrets to life high in his tower, free from the chaos below. And soon, he would have the secrets to the afterlife.

Grey had signed up for cryopreservation a couple of months before and had become progressively more obsessed with the concept of extending one's life past its natural due date. An issue that had irked him upon visiting the facility was the lockers. Each package comes with one locker, the size of a cubic foot, for your post sentimental items, no exceptions. No solution for the wealth after death issue, and nobody else seemed to care about it. Today he remembered visiting those lockers so clearly, and the contract that he flicked through before signing - how one clause had in bold above it: "Please read before dying".

His laptop beeped and Grey startled, an excited buzz racing up his spine.

The transfer was successful. The Arcanum logo rotated smartly on his laptop screen confirming his new account. Below that were the most important twelve words of Grey's life, the seed phrase. Whoever had this seed phrase had his wealth.

Route. Wing. Oven. Addition. Hole. Carpenter. Sink. Cattle. Position. Channel. Chance. Page.

Comically nonsensical and simple.

"Right," he finished his drink in one long, triumphant drag. Time to memorise. The first two were easy enough: 'route' and 'wing'. He thought of a bird, which path would it take? And the next, 'addition' fit nicely with 'hole' if he considered the absence of 'oven' a subtraction. 'Carpenter' and 'sink' almost fit.

You wouldn't call a carpenter to fix your sink, Grey thought. That was something, at least. Then, *the cattle are in the wrong position.* But 'channel' presented a problem. Then 'chance'. As in: *What* chance *do I have of memorising all of this?* And the overwhelming hope that *somehow re-animated Grey and I will end up on the same* page.

Maybe associations weren't the best strategy. Grey spent the better part of an hour pacing his apartment, repeating the words until the syllables timed with his footsteps and they ceased to sound like words at all. He tried a mnemonic device.

"'Read when others are home, cousin,' said Charlie. "Please, can Cat play?" whispered Grey, his teeth grinding on his colleagues' names. It was a supreme irony, but at least Grey knew he would never forget them. He figured it was about time Cat and Charlie made themselves useful.

Clunky, but it just might work.

Grey bounced on the balls of his feet, that electric excitement racing through him again. The final piece of the puzzle. The last stop on the roadmap. He'd figured it out. He had guaranteed his success in life, listened to his father, followed the schematic to a T. Great marks, university, company position, make the right investments, buy the right property, present success to be successful. Everything his father wanted for him. Only now he had exceeded the expectations. He would have success over death.

'Read when others are home, cousin,' said Charlie. Please can Cat play?

He shut the laptop with a satisfied *snap* and bounced around the apartment for a moment more, before settling in a leather armchair, unsure what to do next.

Grey approached the window once more to ogle at the people bar-hopping below. Suddenly he craved to be with them. He wanted to be surrounded by the energy of the living.

Route. Wing. Oven. Addition. Hole. Carpenter. Sink. Cattle. Position. Channel. Chance. Page.

He dialled quickly, cutting in as soon as she answered.

"I have news. Will you meet me?" Grey said. He could almost feel her rolling her eyes over the phone.

A pause. "Hawksmoor?"

Grey grinned. "No, Groucho's."

A longer pause. Grey imagined her biting her lip the way she did when she was frustrated. It was a small thing, really. Sally hated Groucho's. Hated the pretentious cocktails and parquet flooring. Hated the lush draperies and the way the tables were tucked into private little nooks and crannies with chic leather stools instead of chairs. Sally hated stools. Sally wanted to be seen. But when Grey imagined them having this conversation, he pictured them tucked into one of those little nooks. How she would look at him, dark eyes filled with awe, speechless, wine in hand. It just had to be Groucho's.

"C'mon, Sal," he pressed. "Drinks on me."

A sigh. "Fine. Thirty minutes."

Grey glanced at his watch. 8:34. "Twenty-five?"

TWO

Sally Johnson glided across the room in a rush of cashmere and leather boots. She was a kind of painfully, obvious beautiful that would have been somehow more striking on magazines and screens that it was on the streets of London. With her wide brown eyes, full lips, and glossy sheet of dark hair - hair that she had trimmed up to her collarbone, Grey noted with a hint of distaste. He preferred long hair on women, though he had to admit the shorter style enhanced Sally's features.

"You made it," he rose from his seat and leaned over to kiss her on the cheek and let her fresh citrusy scent wash over him. It reminded him of an evening they spent together in late autumn, drinking a bottle of wine on a blanket on the floor and pretending it was a picnic. They played drinking games and stayed up all night telling secrets and kissing and giggling like school kids.

Sally rolled her eyes but accepted the gesture.

"Am I late?"

"Just barely," said Grey.

"What's this?" Sally asked, sliding into her seat, and gesturing to the glass of wine.

"Cabernet," said Grey. "I have another one coming for you in 15 minutes." *Thirteen minutes now.* Grey took a sip of his own wine.

Sally bit her lip and swirled the dark liquid in her glass. "Thanks."

"You look great, Sal," said Grey. She really did. Even with her shorn hair. Sally had a way of looking perfect for every occasion. She was a master of presentation, even during a last-minute drink with an ex, with her elegant blouse unbuttoned just the right amount and flouncy silk print skirt, not a hair out of place. He imagined her in pyjamas on her couch when he called. The way she must have raced to dress for him.

"Thank you for meeting me,"

Sally sipped her wine delicately, licking her bottom lip clean.

"I'm surprised you had time in your schedule,"

"I've always got time for you," said Grey.

"Sure you do," said Sally. Grey noticed that her cheeks had blushed a lovely pink. She smiled at him wryly.

"What are you implying?" he asked. Was he riling her up on purpose? He wasn't sure. Part of him loved arguing with her. Loved the way her lips flushed, and her fists clenched. There was something impossibly sexy about a woman as unflappable as Sally losing it.

She leaned towards him across the table, eyes glinting. "How late was I, Graham?"

Grey swallowed, eyes caught flitting between her lips and her neck. He knew better than to answer though. He just smiled and sipped his wine.

"You and your planning," said Sally after a moment. "You don't have time for people who don't play nice."

"You don't play nice?"

"With all your plans? Historically, no," said Sally. "If I recall correctly, that's why we broke up."

Grey considered this a moment. Then he said, "Was it? I thought you hated the apartment."

"I didn't hate the apartment," said Sally with a snort. "It just didn't fit."

"Didn't fit? What didn't fit? The ring?" Grey asked. He was riling her up on purpose.

"The *life*," said Sally. "Your work, your apartment, your money - there wasn't any room for me."

"Of course there's room. It's a huge apartment," Grey winked.

Sally's knuckles were white around the stem of her glass. Grey felt her eyes searching his face, watched her gaze soften. She sighed. "It is good to see you, Grey. You look good too. Happy."

"I am happy," Grey grinned back at her. "I figured it out, Sal."

The words didn't seem to register at first. Sally stared at him; eyes narrowed in a perplexed squint. Then, finally, it dawned on her, and there it was: that look of wonder he had imagined.

"'Read when others are home, cousin,' said Charlie. Please, can Cat play," said Grey, mostly to prove to himself that he could.

Sally blinked at him. "What?"

"It's a seed phrase, my solution. I've found a way for us to re-animate with wealth," said Grey triumphantly. "That's how we'll do it, cryptos."

"Wow," breathed Sally. "That's—"

"Amazing?" said Grey. "Jeffrey and I worked it all out. We're going to have everything, Sal. A second life, my money - it's all coming together."

Sally seemed shaken by the whole conversation, which was to be expected. It was, at its core, a morbid topic in a lot of ways. She picked up her wine as if to take a sip and seemed to think better of it.

"That's very impressive," she said, finally. "Congratulations."

"Thank you." Grey finished his drink and motioned to the waiter, noting with distaste that according to his watch their second round should have arrived five minutes ago.

"I couldn't imagine it," said Sally after a moment. Her voice was so soft that Grey could barely hear it over the bar noises. "Living forever, I mean."

"No?" asked Grey.

"No," said Sally. "I just - everybody you know will be gone. Doesn't that make you sad?"

Grey thought of James's nasally *'vol-uh-ty-el'* and rumpled his nose. "Not really."

Sally was incredulous. "You'll be all alone, though."

Grey swirled the wine in his glass, watched the liquid spin smoothly as he considered. "You could come," he said softly.

"I could?" Sally gaped.

"Come. Yes," said Grey. He reached across the table and clasped her free hand. "You should come. Maybe it'll be a better fit this time. A bigger apartment,"

"Graham,"

"Just think about it," said Grey. Sally's hand was warm and familiar in his and he was liking the idea more and more as he thought about it. In fact, he was certain that he had always been thinking about it deep down.

planning for it all along. "Think of everything we'll experience, Sal. It's the ultimate adventure..."

"No," said Sally, her voice hard and flat. She pulled her hand free. Grey's hand felt cold in her absence.

Grey blinked. "No?"

"No," Sally said again.

"Why not?" Grey asked. "I can afford the vitrification package for both of us. It's actually pretty affordable to just add you to my plan."

"It's not about your money," she snapped. The colour was back in her cheeks and her lip was red where she bit it.

"Then what is it about?"

"Why do you want me to come?" she countered.

"Well, I mean-," Grey paused, flustered. How was he supposed to answer that? "I just..."

"You have no idea why you want the things you want," said Sally. "You don't even know *what* you want. I'm just a puzzle piece to you."

"Sal..." he rolled his shoulder - a nervous habit - feeling the click in his collarbone.

"Don't 'Sal' me," she snapped. "It's true. You're sitting here talking about your future and your legacy as if I could be part of it, but you're not really seeing me, or what I want."

"I see you just fine," said Grey. "I'm looking right at you."

"No, Grey," said Sally. "You're seeing a link in a chain. You're seeing an asset that you want to bring into your next life. You're checking off items on a list. 'Money, check. Companion, check.' You're not seeing me. You never were."

Grey frowned. At that moment she was a stranger to him. A beautiful woman on the other side of the table, alien features awash in candlelight, blinking curiously up at him. "I don't understand. I thought..."

"You thought what? That I was sitting around waiting for your call? That I would jump at the chance to drop everything and follow you into the after-after life?"

"Is this because you're scared?"

"I'm not scared," Sally tossed her hair angrily. "I just told you that I don't want to live forever."

"Yes," said Grey. "But I don't understand why. You're saying that I don't see you, but I'm looking right at you. You're my Sal. Of course I want you with me."

Sally's dark eyes searched his for a long moment. "Graham," she began. "How late was I?" her voice was soft again.

"It doesn't matter."

"How late?"

Grey felt his teeth grinding together again. "Two and a half minutes."

"Exactly," said Sally. "Do you realise that you haven't gone more than five minutes without glancing at that watch of yours?"

He hadn't, but he wasn't about to admit that.

"You're sitting across the table from me but you're not really here, Grey," she said. "If you were, you would remember that I hate this bar."

"I know that," Grey jumped at this opportunity. "I know it's not your favourite, but there's more privacy and it's much quieter…"

"Do not sit here telling me why I'm wrong to hate this place," Sally seethed. "You chose this bar because *you* like it. When you played out this moment in your head we were here, so here we are. Because you're so fixated on the idea of this perfect life you're setting up for yourself. But it's so hollow, Grey. Don't you see that? You cut out anything that doesn't benefit the plan."

"I thought you would be excited…"

"You thought I would be impressed," corrected Sally.

Grey fidgeted in his seat, wondering how the conversation had gone so wrong. He fought the urge to check his watch - a nervous tick, not some compulsive obsession like Sally seemed to be implying. Sally regarded him coolly from across the table and suddenly Grey hated the dim lighting that somehow sharpened her features. His drink was too sweet and his back hurt from perching on those god-awful stools and all he wanted was to backtrack somehow. To rewind time and watch her walk in again and change the script this time. If he could just figure out the script.

It's so hollow, Grey. Don't you see that?

How could it be true? His perfect job, his beautiful apartment, his entire life in perfect order. Impeccably managed and groomed into the sort of existence most people could only dream of. What could possibly be missing?

It's so hollow.

He couldn't speak. There was a terrible ache in his chest replacing the electric excitement of the day and he found himself staring at the door. A couple entered in a tangle of limbs and laughter, the woman stumbling slightly in her spindly heels. The man caught her waist in an easy, practised move. A kind of casual, possessive intimacy that felt invasive to watch. The man righted his date and flipped the collar of her coat down, bending to kiss her.

"Grey? Are you kidding?" Sally's incredulity pulled Grey back to the table.

"What?" Grey said rather stupidly.

"Are you listening to me at all?" asked Sally, her jaw clenched so tightly that Grey could barely hear her.

"Sal-,"

"You know what, forget it," Sally snapped. She slid from her stool, scooping her clutch up from the table. "Congratulations, Grey. That's what you came to hear and now you've heard it, so…"

"You're not leaving?"

"I am," said Sally, pulling her coat over her shoulders.

"You haven't finished your wine."

"I'm fine," she said.

"You really ought to finish it, you know. They opened the bottle for us. It was expensive…"

"I. Don't. Drink. Cabernet," Sally hissed through clamped teeth. She spun on her heel and stormed out.

Grey sat alone at the table for a long while, sipping his wine contemplatively. He stared at Sally's empty seat, twirling his glass back and forth between his fingers. The ache in his chest was fading as the minutes away from Sally ticked by and he realised that it was never about her at all. Really, when she left the table Grey hadn't felt anything more than frustration at her judgements and relief that he didn't have to listen to her lecture anymore. In fact, what he felt was close to nothing.

Genetics, perhaps. Grey remembered his father feeling similarly when his mother asked for a divorce. Maybe the Wright men were simply less sentimental than most. That didn't mean Grey's life was *hollow*.

He finished his drink, tossed two twenties on the table, and started to leave. Then he thought better of it and downed Sally's abandoned wine. It *was* expensive, after all.

Outside, the noise of the busy street embraced him like a friend. The rain stopped, leaving glistening puddles on the road that sang as cars raced by. Grey started his walk home, glancing at his watch and then scolding himself when he imagined Sally watching him. 10:17.

He shook the image of her out of his head. There was no point in dwelling. What was done was done. Grey sighed and fumbled with his headphones, fingers stiff and clumsy with alcohol. He wove through the stream of pedestrians, dodging splashes of dirty street water when the cars flitted by. He was untying a particularly difficult knot in one of his headphone wires when several things happened at once.

A woman flicked her cigarette.

A jogger veered to avoid the flying ember, slipping slightly on the damp street and colliding with Grey, who was fixated on his headphones.

A wrench of pain as Grey's foot slipped, ankle rolling painfully off the curb, and he fell into the river of cars.

A blinding light and a screech of tires as the lorry tried in vain to stop.

And a watch shattered on the street. 10:19.

THREE

Time stopped seeming so linear.

"BP 89 over 60," screamed the ambulance technician over the wail of the siren as it rushed down the street. Grey blinked and the walls of the ambulance blurred-

"I donated a lot of money to this hospital, and I want to see..." Grey's father's voice echoed down the hospital hallway. Grey wished he would stop yelling. His head was splitting.

In the ambulance: "O neg. No, the other one. Jesus Christ kid, is it your first day?" The technician shook his head. Grey couldn't feel his legs. He needed to tell somebody that he couldn't feel his-

"Well, what was he doing playing in the bloody street?" His father shouted at somebody, but Grey couldn't quite-

"Oh, Graham…" Sally, tear-streaked and sobbing. He opened his mouth to say something, anything to comfort her, but he wasn't in his body anymore, and yet he was only a body and it hurt, everything was hurting, make it stop hurting-

It's so hollow, Grey. Don't you see that?

"Come on, buddy, hang on now. We're almost there," back in the ambulance and Grey couldn't breathe, his lungs were full of fire and his legs-

"Group Delta-A Mark 317," A different place. Quiet and cold.

"I don't give a shit about a DNR," His father's eyes were bloodshot and watery. Grey worried he wasn't sleeping enough.

"Has someone called the vitrification place?" murmured a voice that sounded like Jeff.

A dark place. Grey could hear beeping machines, felt the prick of an IV. Somebody murmuring softly.

"As soon as we declare death, you understand? The fresher the better,"

In the ambulance: "He's a goner. I mean, look at him,"
In the hospital: Horrible, primal sobs heaving from Grey's father.
The quiet place: "Sequence locked. Let's bring 'em back."
A dark place: "Time of death, 2:07am. Vitrification commencing,"
And then cold and quiet and-

*

"Good morning, Graham. Why don't you open your eyes for me?"

The voice undulated as if its speaker was underwater. Grey ignored it.

There was a light overhead. Grey could feel the warmth of it on his cheek. He ruminated on the sensation for a while.

I must be lying down, he thought, though that didn't really make sense. Lying down meant he had a body - did he have a body? He thought he remembered touch, pressure, and heat, but now there was only warmth. His entire existence narrowed down to the prickling heat on his cheek and the cool metal at his back. Cold. As he lay, there was a strange, almost inflating, sensation. Grey imagined this to be how a butterfly felt in its cocoon, limbs and wing crystallising around him, bringing him into existence.

Smell came next. Something thick and vaguely antiseptic that burned Grey's nose. And yet, beneath that, citrus and floral. The scent tickled something in his head, a memory-

"Open your eyes,"

The voice was sharpening and with it came the rumble of other sounds. Clicks and beeps and footsteps pressing in on him painfully. The pressure in his ear drums building until Grey was certain his head would split in two. His mouth filled with the taste of copper. He could feel his heart beating erratically in his chest, the pulse of blood gathering in his palms. He tried to cover his ears, desperate to block out the sensation. It was too much, the cold bite of metal at his back, the light burning him, machinery whirring, the memory of his father's sobs, the voice urging him to open his eyes, more voices shouting out strings of numbers that he couldn't understand.

Grey opened his eyes.

His vision swam and blurred. The ceiling was an indiscernible mass of silver above him. Faceless white shapes circled him, close enough to touch if he could only move his arms.

"That's good, Graham." said the voice. He blinked twice and the room slowly floated into focus. A warehouse, silver tubes and a mass of wiring snaked above him. Giant stacked machines screeched and beeped, lights flashed. The voice must have come from one of the dozen masked people shuffling around his bed. People decked in some sort of plasticky white material that resembled a hazmat suit, their faces hidden behind reflective screens so Grey could see his own terrified eyes when they looked at him.

He opened his mouth - to cry, or maybe to shout for somebody, Sally perhaps, but nothing happened. His eyes darted dizzily, seeking out a familiar face. Where was his father? He wanted his father.

"Heart rate 143 beats per minute," said a suit standing by one of the mysterious machines. "And rising."

"Graham," said the voice coming from the suit nearest to him. "I'm going to need you to take a deep breath."

But Grey couldn't. He couldn't process what the voice was saying at all. He had caught a glimpse of himself in the suit's mask. He had a clear picture of the tubes braided into his chest, into his neck, into his arms and legs. Pumping some dark liquid into his body. Into his blue, lifeless limbs, inflating before his eyes like macabre water balloons.

"154," said the second suit.

"He's crashing," shouted another.

Grey heard a rattling over the roar of blood in his ears. His heart was surely about to burst free from his chest. The dark, sludgy liquid would ooze out of him like an overfed tick bursting. His stomach gave a nauseous lurch. Grey gagged, immediately aware that there was nothing in his stomach for him to expel. The rattling was him, he realised. His body was shaking violently against the metal bed frame.

"You need to relax," said the voice. Grey felt pressure on his arm. The suit was touching him.

"160!"

Grey opened his mouth again and let out a strangled howl.

"Gas him!"

Something was placed over his face, obscuring his vision and Grey felt another bolt of panic. Were they sending him back to the dark place? There was a hissing sound and the smell of lavender and lemons.

"Good, good!" said the voice. "Just breathe, just breathe."

This time Grey complied, taking in great gulps of the sweet-smelling air as his body ceased its shaking. His heart slowed and the horror of his body faded to something like objective curiosity. The icy cold on his back faded to comfortably cool and he wondered if his senses were dulling or if the dark liquid was warming him.

"There he is!" the voice sounded pleased.

"Heart rate falling, 76 beats per minute."

"It should be lower with his composition," the voice replied. "Let me know when it hits 60."

"Copy," said the second suit.

"Platelet levels are normal," said a third suit looking down at a strange round device in their hand. Someone removed the breathing apparatus from Grey's face.

"Good," said the voice. "Your vision is 20/20, correct?"

This was directed at Grey who rasped out a quiet "Yes…"

"How are we doing on hydro?" the voice asked.

"92%," said another suit.

"Excellent."

Grey's throat felt like it was lined with sawdust, but he forced himself to speak. "Where am I?"

The suits ignored him, bustling around machines, turning dials, and adjusting tubes.

"Heart rate 60."

"Hydration threshold reached."

"BP 118 over 80."

Grey tried again. "What's going on?"

The suits sprang into action, unhooking the monitors and tubes from his body in perfect synchronisation. His sedation had him floating in a boneless state of fuzzy relaxation.

"Welcome back, Mr. Wright," said the voice when they were done. "The film will explain everything."

Grey could only blink stupidly at his own reflection in the mask, completely immobile save for his eyes. The suit on his right held the round device over his head, which beeped twice. The suits seemed to glean great meaning from this. The voice squeezed Grey's shoulder in what was surely supposed to be a comforting gesture.

They wheeled him away from the swathe of machines. Grey glanced out of the corner of his eye and saw several machine banks identical to his own with their own team of suits and tubes and dark liquid. He wondered what kind of hospital he was in. Possibly an overflow station?

He heard a door open, and the warehouse ceiling became the panelled ceiling of a dimly lit hallway. Intermittent sconces threw round pools of light above him. Grey counted twenty-two light pools before he heard another door open, and he was wheeled into a large room with a much taller ceiling. There was a smooth whir of machinery and his bed folded, raising his upper body into a sitting position. The suits shuffled out with a rasp of plastic and Grey was left in the partial darkness to observe his surroundings.

It took him only a moment to realise he was in some sort of cinema. He was facing the great white projection screen, seated slightly centre left. There was something foreign about the room. Perhaps it was simply because the chairs had been removed to make space for the beds, but there was something old-fashioned about the aesthetic. It reminded him of going to the movies as a child, and yet - there was no scent of popcorn in the air, no sweet-mildewed scent of spilt fizzy drinks on the floor. His eyes were telling him he was in a cinema, but his other senses knew better.

The thought might have bothered him, but his head was still floating in the haze of his sedation. And he wasn't alone. Out of the corner of his eye he could just make out the silvery metal beds and human shapes beside him. Five, maybe six others. Grey wondered, passively, if they knew any more about what was going on than he did. He was just working up the courage to open his mouth, but the lights dimmed even further, and the screen lit up.

The picture opened on a sweeping shot of a field dotted with wildflowers and set below a sweeping, pearly blue sky. A river babbled softly in the background and a breeze just kissed the grass, sending rippling sheens of green across the foreground. In the corner of the screen, a black and white animated character danced, a retro-futuristic Jetson-style housewife from the 1950s.

"Reanimation and You!" the crisp female voice said with a New York accent as the words appeared on the screen. "Good morning, and welcome to the 23rd century!"

Grey felt a jolt of panic shocking him even through his haze. The jogger, the lorry, the ambulance - he had done it. Vitrification and reanimation. He heard one of his neighbours shift beside him, probably having the same realisation. The narrator seemed prepared for this moment of belated understanding and the shot stayed static for a moment. If he had been able to move his arms, Grey might have wrapped them around himself. Had he not been drugged, he suspected he would start shaking again.

After a while the shot continued to follow the stream as the narrator spoke. Grey wondered if they had chosen the soft lapping sounds purposefully to put the newly reanimated at ease. He was pretty sure it was effective, though it might have been the sedation.

"A lot has changed since you've been asleep!" said the narrator, and the picture shifted. Pristine white marble buildings dotting beautifully manicured green spaces. They seemed to have engineered their cities around nature in a way that blended the buildings into the landscape. The result was breath-taking. Families gathered in the green, eating and laughing together. The sky was an unnatural shade of blue filled with puffy white clouds. It looked like a painting.

"Humanity has evolved," said the narrator. "We have created a society that sits perfectly in balance with nature. We are just one cog in a wheel that includes every living being on this planet, and therefore must be meticulous in our protection of the environment."

The movie cycled through idyllic shots of humans interacting with the environment. Treehouses that were really hydroponic green houses built into the skyline, the water waste feeding the trees below. Crystal clear lakes and streams. Oceans and reefs exploding with life. Grey blinked with a sudden realisation. There were no cars. No roads. The impossible blues and greens on the screen weren't enhanced. He was looking at a world with no pollution.

"The human race changed its perspectives for good after the Great Environmental Collapse, and of course, the 4th World War. People turned their sights away from the wasteful society of the past, choosing instead to value preservation, education and creativity."

The shot shifted again, this time to a concert hall, an amphitheatre built into a natural outdoor crater. A woman sang, her voice ringing gorgeous and clear, while a group watched on in delight. A sculpture carved a gossamer thread into a marble statue. Painters scraped riots of colours across canvasses. Actors rehearsed a play.

"The world has healed..." said the narrator. More shots of clean waters, pristine mountains, and lush greenery. "And now you've healed too!" Another sweeping shot, this time over a building that seemed to be carved out of a cliffside.

"Some time after your vitrification process, the company that froze your body was dissolved, and your body was purchased by MerryCom, a professional services conglomerate with a vested interest in the extension of human life."

The camera zoomed in on the building, noting the MerryCom logo above the door.

"MerryCom stored your body by utilising the most advanced technology and ecological safety practices to develop the Ark."

Cut to a building diagram, revealing a long shaft leading down to a massive chamber, deep underground.

"The Ark is a self-sustaining ecosystem that uses power from the Earth's core to store bodies at the optimal temperature for preservation," continued the narrator. "Congratulations on your selection! With a society as carefully balanced as ours, the choice to reanimate an individual is no small one. You have been chosen as an important cog in this green-machine."

Grey felt a creeping sense of anxiety. Was this some sort of orientation video?

"Entering society can be a difficult transition. Thankfully, MerryCom has developed an exceptional program that will allow you to work off your storage debt and revival tax while you develop the tools and skills needed to integrate into our beautiful society."

Cue a shot of a man sweeping a hallway with a smile plastered on his face. Above his head a countdown read '4 years'.

"Most debts are paid within 5-20 years depending on the value of the work provided. You will be issued a release date formulated from the debt accumulated from your purchase, maintenance fee in the Ark, and the revival tax based on the carbon impact of your former life. We understand this information can be overwhelming, but it is necessary to maintain our zero-waste society."

The camera shifted back to the idyllic city shots. Grey watched on with a continued prickling sense of unease. He wondered when he would be allowed to speak to a person, and how much a year of what amounted to involuntary servitude was worth. The vitrification and reanimation were successful. Grey could only hope his other scheme had worked as well.

"After your balance is paid, you will integrate into society. In exchange for your hard work, you will be provided with full immunisations and vaccinations, as well as, of course, any repairs that your body needs from before the freeze! You will be provided with a home, food, and full access to healthcare. After integration, most reanimated individuals report great satisfaction with their place in society."

"Welcome back, once again, from MerryCom to you!" said the narrator. A kitschy little jingle played as the camera swooped over the MerryCom headquarters and across the green landscape beyond.

Grey's head was buzzing again. His vision swirled in and out of focus with every blink. He glanced around hurriedly, searching for anybody to explain his situation to now that the film was ending. But he couldn't make anything out. In fact, the room was dimming. There was a great rush of dizziness and Grey felt himself slip into darkness once more.

FOUR

A sharp jolt raced up Grey's fingers, waking him. This time, his eyes flew open immediately. He was in another antiseptic white room surrounded by machines. To his left, a mask-less suit fiddled with a long, pointed metal instrument. Grey was staring, momentarily shocked to take in the first human face he had seen since waking up in the 23rd century.

The man was older than Grey, though not by much. Grey guessed that he was in his forties, with silvering dark hair and a faint splatter of wrinkles around his deep-set eyes. He was long-limbed and lanky. The plasticky material of his suit gaped around his thinness.

"Hello," Grey's voice was less hoarse now, but it still felt strange. He supposed that was what happened when one didn't speak for about two hundred years.

The man didn't look up but continued to manipulate the instrument in his hand. "I was wondering when you'd wake up," his voice was rich and deep. "You slept through your legs..."

At that, Grey returned his attention to the metal instrument. As he watched, the man pressed a button at the top of the device and out slid a needle that was so feathery thin that Grey could just barely see it. The man slid the needle into Grey's arm and Grey winced, more out of anticipation than discomfort. He could barely feel it at all. There was a soft humming sound and what felt like liquid fire raced up his arm. The muscles in his arm spasmed and twitched to life as the fire dissipated. Grey stared at his arm in wonder as the man withdrew the needle, flexing his fingers gingerly.

"What *was* that?" Grey asked.

"You're from the 21st century, yeah?" said the man.

"I am," said Grey.

"Did you ever jump start a car battery?"

Grey blanched. The man inserted the needle higher into Grey's bicep. This time Grey braced himself for the fire.

"I'm Dr. Simonds," said the man. "And you are Graham Wright. 33 years old, 80.73 kilograms, 182.88 centimetres, 18% body fat - nice work by the way, a lot of Rainies lose tone in storage, but you held up quite nicely,"

"Thank you?" said Grey, though he supposed it was more luck than skill on his part.

"You're a quiet one," said Dr. Simonds. "Normally people talk my ear off, asking questions, crying, confused, that sort of thing,"

Grey shrugged. "Just overwhelmed, I guess,"

Dr. Simonds nodded sagely. "That's to be expected. I must say, you handle it better than most. I had a woman in here, about a month ago, just crying. Crying so hard that I couldn't keep her still to finish waking her up, you know? Well, I get her talking, calmed her down a bit. Eventually come to find out, her husband set up the reanimation for both of them and didn't tell her! She had no idea what was going on. I mean, who would expect it, right? And then, get this, the poor bastard wasn't even selected to come back. He's in a locker somewhere and his poor wife is hysterical asking about St. Peter and the pearly gates," Dr. Simonds shook his head and withdrew the needle device from Grey's neck.

"That's hideous," said Grey, tilting his head this way and that, marvelling at the ability to move. "I guess I'm lucky, in that regard. Planned for it myself."

Dr. Simonds moved on to Grey's right arm. "Some people still forget. Sign the papers and get distracted with life I suppose."

Grey laughed. "Not me. I, er, *died*, I guess right after I set this thing up,"

"Let's hope your luck doesn't follow you into this life," said Dr. Simonds with a snort.

"Cheers," Grey agreed, wincing as Dr. Simonds zapped his shoulder back to life.

"Excellent," said the Doctor. "I don't quite understand the selection criteria for how they pick you 21st-century Rainies... the Ark is full of the extremely elderly, and it doesn't make sense to reanimate many of those, but it still happens, usually just as someone to hold a gun. Younger bodies, like your own, are harder to come by... something about how not many young people could afford it. Could you stand for me, Mr. Wright?"

Grey swung his legs from the gurney with careful, tentative movements and slid to his feet. To his surprise his body responded effortlessly. He marvelled at his own weight, shifting from one foot to the other, stretching his arms overhead, cracking his knuckles one by one. Perfect. He was perfect. He rolled his shoulder carefully, waiting for the tell-tale click of his collar bone, but there was nothing. He stared at Dr. Simonds in wonder.

"We fixed your eyesight too," Dr. Simonds said, laying the silver instrument on a tray and reaching for a shorter, blunter device.

"I had perfect vision," Grey said, eyeing the device warily.

"Nearly perfect," said Dr. Simonds with a wink. "Arms out please."

Grey complied, stretching his arms out at his sides. Dr. Simonds examined the device in his hands, frowning slightly. Grey felt a prick of unease.

"Everything okay, Doctor?"

"Perfectly," said Dr. Simonds. "Wingspan, 184 centimetres."

The marvel of his working limbs wearing off, Grey returned his attention to the matter at hand. "While I've got you here, is there a compu-," but a shrill beep cut off his words. A screen that Grey hadn't noticed because it blended so perfectly with the wall behind it lit up red and words scrolled across: *Relocation Office.*

"Just in time," said the Doctor. "Don't be nervous. Well-built guy like you? You'll get something good, debt-free in five,"

"Actually that's-,"

"Sit down again for me, please"

Dr. Simonds pressed another button on the device in his hand and once again Grey's nose was full of lavender and lemons. His vision wavered. *So much for perfect,* he thought before the world faded to black once more.

*

Gone were the sterile hospital walls and foreign instruments. This time Grey awoke to the sounds of chaos. There was an acrid smell of smoke and something coppery sweet. He had the sensation of moving very fast, like the first drag of an airplane taking off. He opened his eyes and found that he was on what appeared to be some sort of windowless train. Leather straps across his chest lashed him upright to his seat. Once again, he was not alone. His companions were in various states of awareness, some sitting grim-faced and stoic, others mirroring Grey with their bleary, confused blinking.

"Good morning, sunshine," said a gravelly voice. Before Grey could take stock of the man standing before him, a heavy vest made from hard and flexible material was thrust into his arms. "Put it on," the man moved on to the next seat.

Grey shrugged on the vest, zipping it up to his chin. He met the eyes of a woman across the aisle. She looked young, certainly younger than him, with wispy blonde hair piled on top of her head. Her lips were thin and white, and she stared back at him with unreadable hazel eyes. Grey swallowed hard. There was an anxious pit in his stomach. He looked away.

"Take it."

This time it was a gun thrust into his lap. Grey blinked at it as his hands closed around the unfamiliar weight. "If you see anyone not dressed like us, use it. Make it to the morning and we'll talk."

"I- I don't-," *know how to use this,* he would have said, but the transport shuddered to a stop. Grey was forced to his feet and shoved in line with the others. The transport walls rattled as they slid open, and Grey was pushed off of the ledge into the mud below.

This was not the utopian green cityscape the orientation film had promised. This was hell. Mud up to his ankles, with little makeshift fabric shanties propped up here and there, looming out of the smoke and mist that gathered and swirled and burned the back of Grey's throat. It was night, either that or the sun was blocked out with the thick smoke that surrounded him. He blinked, trying to squint through the darkness. There was a flash of light and a sound like thunder. A heavy thud. Then screaming.

"Get down!" a rough hand dragged Grey down into the dirt. He couldn't make out its owner. The transport doors had slid shut as it disappeared over the horizon, taking its light with it. There was something soft to his left. He turned his head and squinted. Another flash of light rocketed overhead. It was the woman from the transport, blonde hair coated with mud, wide eyes framing a bullet hole in her forehead.

Grey scrambled away. This was warfare.

The realisation seemed to inject a jolt of adrenaline in his veins. Lights were flashing overhead, it sounded like the very world itself was tearing at the seams, he needed cover. He crawled, mouth filling with mud and blood and grime, but he didn't care. The world had narrowed. He was a creature of breath and heartbeat and instinct. Freezing as the light flashed overhead, scrambling in the darkness, gun forgotten, ears buzzing with the overwhelming roar, and the earth was shaking under his fingers, a great dark shape lurching out of the mist and smoke. *Tank,* he thought, though it didn't look like any sort of machinery he was familiar with. It was all smooth metal and rounded edges as it barrelled towards him. He threw himself to the side, rolling down an embankment and away from the screeching metal.

Grey thumped to a stop at the bottom of a rocky depression in the earth. There was a harsh rattling sound, which he quickly realised was his breathing. Another flash of light and three sets of luminous eyes appeared in the darkness. Grey clambered back until he hit a rock wall, gagging on adrenaline, cursing the impossibility that for all his efforts he was going to die here, at the bottom of a trench.

More light overhead. This time Grey could make out the vests, identical to his own. He looked and let out a laugh that was probably closer to a sob or a wail, then lowered his head into his shaking hands.

"It wasn't supposed to be like this,"

Grey raised his head and squinted at the speaker. A man, a man far too old to be in a firefight. Truly, Grey wondered how he had made it this far. He sat shaking and sobbing, wiry arms wrapped around his narrow chest, white hair barely visible in the darkness, looking so frail and feeble that Grey felt a wave of revulsion. Grey pressed the back of his hand into his mouth to stifle his laugh, wondering if this was what shock felt like.

"Chin up," said a woman. She was so thoroughly coated in mud that Grey hadn't noticed her until she'd opened her eyes.

"I- I wish-," sobbed the old man. "They should have left me. I wish they'd left me-,"

"On the transport?" asked Grey, surprising himself with how steadily the words came out.

The old man shook his head and turned to Grey with milky blue eyes. "Dead," he said. He began rocking himself back and forth and Grey was reminded perversely of a mother rocking a cradle.

"You don't mean that." said the woman so softly Grey wasn't sure he had heard her at all.

"They should have kept me dead. I want to be dead," the old man howled. He lunged suddenly, scraping his way up the embankment with the agility of a much younger man.

"No-!" the woman screamed, scrambling for the old man.

But he was already out of reach, over the embankment, back in the mud and smog. There was a flash of light, a crack like a whip, and the old man collapsed screaming and clutching his leg.

Grey didn't know what made him do it. He was out of his mind. The shock and the chaos warped his judgement, sent him scrambling up the embankment after the old man. His hands found the old man thrashing in the dark. He howled and the sound set off goosebumps on Grey's skin. Grey gripped him under the armpits and dragged him. He was heavier than he looked and worse than dead weight with all of his flailing. Still, Grey dragged him as quickly as he could manage, gritting his teeth with the effort.

For a moment Grey thought the old man had hit him. There was a pressure on his shoulder and suddenly Grey was on his back looking up at the sky.

What happened?

Grey touched his shoulder with a trembling hand, his fingers coming back thick with blood. And then Grey felt it, the torn muscles, the shattered bone where the bullet had ripped him apart. The stars seemed to flicker and stir above him shot through with fingers of mist from the ground below. Grey opened his mouth and roared into the night, the sound swallowed by the screams and bullets.

FIVE

"That's the last you remember?"

Grey tore his gaze away from his shaking hands and studied his counsellor. They had met twice previously; the first time so she could explain that he had survived his time on the front lines, the second so she could inform him of the two-year credit they were offering him as compensation for his injury, and now the third meeting where she marched him painfully through the memory of it all. These meetings were the only respite from the cell he slept in. She was eyeing him coolly through a pair of black-rimmed glasses that Grey suspected were for effect only. He imagined a society that could bring people back from the dead with no hint of their previous ailments probably had little need for bifocals. She spun her pen in her fingers absently and Grey noted that pens hadn't much changed in the last few hundred years. He had a sudden flash of Sally, hair bunned on the top of her head and pinned through with a pencil while she made pancakes for them both.

He cleared the sudden tightness in his throat. "Yes. The old man, the gunshot, and then it goes black," He didn't ask the obvious question, though his voice broke slightly remembering the man's blood - his screams.

She seemed to sense where his thoughts had led him. His counsellor's mouth set into a thin line. "He was an unfortunate casualty,"

Grey's teeth ground together painfully, and he clenched his fists, wincing as his shoulder complained. When he awoke after the battlefield, his shoulder had been healed. Only a small star-shaped scar hinted at the injury. Strangely, he could still feel something aching deep in the muscle. Like whatever magic they used to fix him only went so deep and a wound festered below.

He couldn't stare at those useless glasses anymore. He busied himself with the room instead. Another antiseptic white room. White walls that Grey was sure held an untold number of screens. Another unlabelled door leading into the labyrinthine and ambiguous Ark. The counsellor perched at a table, flicking her pen back and forth across her fingers while she studied him.

"What's the pen for?" Grey asked.

The counsellor blinked in surprise, placing the pen down on the empty table. "Why do you ask?"

Grey fought the urge to roll his eyes. "No paper," he said. "You've got a pen with nothing to write on. I've seen those little tablet devices you all carry around, and you don't need a pen to take notes."

The counsellor almost looked amused. "Transitional periods can be difficult," she uncrossed and crossed her legs primly. "We try to mitigate some of the discomfort as our patients adjust to the jump in time."

"So, you match our time periods?" said Grey. "You want me to open up, so you come in here with a pen you don't use and glasses you don't need, looking like a therapist from the 21st century?"

"To put you at ease, yes," said the counsellor.

It's so hollow, Grey. Don't you see that?

Grey met her gaze. "You didn't care much about my ease before you suited me up and sent me out for target practice."

She held his stare, mouth tightening. "That was a miscalculation on our part, Mr. Wright,"

"Grey," he corrected.

"Grey," she amended. "Dr. Simonds assumed with your physical prowess a year of military service would be an excellent repayment plan. Unfortunately, your heroics were not enough to make up for your poor performance on the front lines. Further analysis of your stats has shown that you are much better suited for maintenance. You will be transported to the MerryCom facility to begin your tenure. With your injury credit applied to your debt, you will reach repaid status in 11 years,"

"Hold on-," said Grey, rising to his feet in alarm.

"We understand that the allure of a shorter repayment plan can be-,"

"Listen to me. I don't need to be put on a repayment plan at all. I have money," said Grey. "If I could just borrow a computer-,"

"That would be impossible, Mr. Wright," said the counsellor. "MerryCom employees are not allowed to access the open web."

"I'm not an employee," Grey snapped.

"You are."

"And who decided that, huh?" Grey had a sudden urge to kick the wall, to shatter one of their fancy, hidden screens. "I didn't sign up for indentured servitude."

"You signed a clause that says that you are subject to all legislation applicable at which time you are reanimated-,"

"-and the legislation says that I have to pay a carbon tax, I understand," said Grey. "But I am telling you that I have money."

"That's impossible Mr. Wright," the counsellor was disturbingly calm. "MerryCom employees are not allowed,"

Grey wanted to grab her by her birdlike shoulders and shake the tranquillity out of her. "You can access it for me then. I'm telling you I worked it all out. I set aside money-,"

"It has never been legal to retain assets, specifically monetary assets after death," said the counsellor. "I can assure you that any potential descendants have been notified of your status and have not come forward to cover your debt-,"

"I had a loophole," Grey insisted. "Jeffrey - my financial advisor - we set up a crypto wallet with a seed password,"

For the first time, the counsellor frowned. "I don't understand,"

Her confusion was a thread of hope and he clung to it. "It's an online currency. The seed password unlocks it. I can explain everything if you'll just let me access the internet."

The counsellor raised one eyebrow, dark eyes studying Grey for a moment, unreadable. Wordlessly she slid her tablet across the table and Grey lunged for it.

It was smaller than Grey's fist, all rounded edges and cold in his palm. He tapped what he guessed to be the screen: a small iridescent square that barely stood out from the rest of the device. A screen appeared in the air above his fist. Grey marvelled at it for a moment. Visually corporeal and somehow not really there at all, it seemed to shimmer in the air before him. He pulled his focus back to the task at hand with effort.

There were symbols on the shimmering air-screen that Grey didn't recognise, labelled with words that looked like English but meant nothing to him. He was missing cultural context. Two hundred years of changing corporate lingo, slang, and colloquialisms completely lost to him. He decided to take his chances, clicking on a random unrecognisable squiggle. The screen shimmered once again and shifted to a different screen full of different unrecognisable squiggles. Grey grit his teeth again, clicking another symbol at random. Another shift, more symbols.

"Dammit," Grey hissed through his teeth. "Christ, how do I..."

Click, shimmer, unreadable screen. Click, shimmer, unreadable screen.

The counsellor was unmoved. "Mr. Wright," she said calmly. "This is a hopeless endeavour."

Grey ignored her, continuing his tapping. He didn't even know how to back out of whatever application he had opened that was currently beeping loudly and flashing multicoloured lights at him. Where was the home button? Where were any buttons?

"Mr. Wright, please hand over the tablet."

Grey let out a sound somewhere between a scream and a sob. "Why don't you help me?"

"The tablet, Mr. Wright."

"I have money. I'll show you if you'll just help me…"

Click, shimmer, unreadable screen. Grey started to realise that the internet he knew was no more, and likely, his golden ticket out of here with it.

"I can't do that,"

"Then what *can* you do?" Grey roared. "You useless-," he pitched the tablet across the room, injured shoulder screaming in protest, where it shattered against the wall. "-ineffectual garbage."

"That's enough," said the counsellor. "If you cannot get yourself under control-,"

"I want to go back," Grey's chest was heaving. His feet moved frantically around the room. He was trapped in that sterile white room with this sterile white woman, and nobody was coming to his rescue. Nobody alive to remember him, to help him. Nothing. The old man was right. Sally was right. "I need to go back. Put me back,"

"All right, Mr. Wright," said the counsellor. She leaned back and tapped a spot on the wall. "That's enough."

Lavender and lemons and darkness.

SIX

Grey was getting sick of waking up in different places. When he came back to consciousness this time, he waited a few moments, breathing deeply with his eyes closed. He wanted to savour a moment of peace before he faced whatever awaited him in this new location. So, he inhaled and exhaled evenly, clearing the citrus and floral smells from his nose, trying to keep his mind from racing ahead and figuring out his next steps.

After his fourth time imagining suing MerryCom into oblivion, he abandoned the exercise completely. He had never been good at staying in the moment. He was a survivor, a planner. Adapted for a stressful corporate world where success meant staying steps ahead of your opponent. There used to be a map, a clear hierarchy of what capable people did to stay ahead. Now Grey was at a loss. The compass was wrong. He turned right and ended up in the 23rd century.

He sighed heavily and opened his eyes. He was in a small bed tucked into the wall of an even smaller room. More white walls - Grey wondered if MerryCom had ever heard of colour. Light was pouring from an unseen source. Grey wondered if the walls themselves were fluorescent somehow, but they were cool and smooth to his touch. The entire space was about the size of his office at work, with just enough room for the bed, a sink, and a large cloudy plastic tube that ran from floor to ceiling in the corner. Grey covered the whole area in four steps.

He glanced down and realised that they had changed him once again. This time he was in a long-sleeved slate-coloured shirt and a pair of thick dark trousers. He missed his tailored suits. Missed his office and his infuriating co-workers.

"Visitor," said a crisp male voice. The sound seemed to come from everywhere all at once. Grey clapped his hands over his ears, finding the combination of the disembodied voice and light slightly nauseating.

"Visitor," repeated the voice. Grey was at a loss. There was no door that he could see, unless-

He approached the tube in the corner and peeked in, cupping his hands around his eyes like he would if he was looking through a two-way mirror.

"It's a shower."

Grey startled at the voice and spun around. A doorway had appeared on the wall opposite his bed and in the doorway stood a man. He looked older than Grey, early forties maybe, with sandy blonde hair cropped close to his skull. He had a short and powerful build, like somebody who'd spent years on a construction crew. The combination might have been frightening if it weren't for his wide friendly smile. Grey found himself smiling back, noting that his was the first welcoming face he had seen since his reanimation.

"That makes sense," Grey said, stepping away from the apparent shower.

"Does it?" the man's eyes crinkled like somebody who smiled often. Grey wondered distantly if that was another affection put on by MerryCom to comfort him. The man was wearing the same plain shirt and jeans combination as him. Some sort of uniform? He didn't know what was real anymore. Maybe he was paranoid.

"I guess not," Grey admitted, keeping his voice neutral.

"Of course not," said the man with a laugh. "Who expects to shower in a tube?"

Grey fought back a smile. After the horror of the battlefield and the sterility of the doctors and the counsellor, he was having a surprisingly easy time warming to the stranger. It was strange. Grey didn't remember noticing people smiling much in his first life.

"It's not so bad, though. I'm Mark," said the man, extending a hand for Grey to shake. "I'm your buddy."

"Grey." Grey shook his hand gingerly, noting the callouses. Mark definitely wasn't a stranger to labour. "Sorry, you're my what?"

"Orientation buddy," explained Mark. "Part therapist, part spiritual guide, part human resource lackey. I'm here to help you adjust to the exciting world of Labour and Maintenance,"

Grey wasn't sure he needed a therapist or a spiritual guide. Mark let out a bellowing laugh.

"Look at your face, wow. You've got to relax, man. It's just a job,"

Grey rolled his shoulder absently. "Right, a job, sorry. I guess I didn't like the last one they gave me,"

Mark's grin slipped and he regarded Grey thoughtfully. "They told me you came from the lines, horrible business, relocating the slums."

Grey looked away. He could sense a curiosity in Mark's expression, and he had no desire to relive his interview with the counsellor, or those memories yet.

Mark appeared to sense Grey's apprehension. "No worries, man. Anyway, we've got to get a move on. Here's your Chroniker," Mark fastened a watch-like device around Grey's wrist. The face was smaller than a matchbox and featured another mostly invisible screen. When Grey turned his wrist to look at it a tiny projection read '0c'.

"It's mostly useless," continued Mark. "Just keeps track of your credits. Follow me."

Grey followed Mark into the blank white hallway outside, stopping momentarily to watch the door to his room slide back into place behind them and disappear seamlessly into the wall. He stumbled to catch up to Mark, who was already rounding a bend. MerryCom really was a maze, thought Grey as Mark led him through nondescript hallway after nondescript hallway.

"Mind the guards," said Mark in Grey's ear as a pair of black-uniformed men marched past them. Grey noted the familiar shape of a gun strapped to each of their sides. "They mostly leave us alone unless we're causing trouble or slowing productivity."

Grey swallowed, his throat uncomfortably dry. He nodded his confirmation instead.

"The most important thing," said Mark as they climbed a staircase out of what Grey had begun to think of as a dorm. "is not to lose your Chroniker. Really, don't take it off for any reason. It's the only record you have of your credits."

"What are my credits?" asked Grey.

"Your work credits. Time served. And if you lose them, or somebody steals them, they're gone. You have to start all over again, plus the time credits for a new Chroniker." said Mark.

"Are they stolen often?" asked Grey.

"Not if the thief knows what's good for them," said Mark darkly. "It's basically a cardinal sin. I mean, could you look somebody in the eye and steal literal hours of their life?"

"Of course not," he said, ashamed that for a split second he *had* imagined a scenario where he could have. It was in his nature to cheat the system. Anything to come out ahead. His was a scheming brain, after all.

"Good," said Mark. "Besides, it's an impossible crime to get away with. If the Rainies don't get you, the guards will. You don't want to get on the guards' bad side."

"Right," Grey stared at the device, feeling the weight of its importance. Why did MerryCom need so many guards? The comparison to indentured servitude was becoming starkly obvious. "How many credits do you have?"

"Hey, buddy, buy me dinner first," said Mark with a wink. Grey felt a flush of embarrassment. Apparently, sentencing was something of a sensitive subject.

They left the staircase and went through a door into a breezeway overlooking a cliffside on the left and a misty valley to the right. Grey gaped at the view, frozen still. It was like no landscape he had ever seen before. The great rock wall was coarse and veined through with red and blue minerals in the most elaborate tapestry Grey had ever seen. On the right, the valley glowed picturesquely. The greens were greener, the sky bluer, and the misty dew below was a lush purple blanket below the treetops. Looking at the perfection below made the front lines seem like an impossible nightmare.

"Come on," Mark broke Grey from his thoughts. "Don't want to be late on day one."

Grey followed reluctantly, trying to catch a glimpse of the valley long after they finished crossing the breezeway and made their way into another blank white hallway.

"Was that real?" Grey asked.

"Was what real?"

"The valley, the cliff, all of it."

Mark laughed. "Of course."

"What about the rest of it?"

"The rest of what?"

"The *world*," said Grey, with a flush of frustration. "It can't all be like that - so perfect. Right? What's it like outside?"

"I, er-," Mark paused for a moment, considering. "Well, I don't really know if I'm the best person to comment. Labour and Maintenance personnel don't typically leave the facility all that much."

"Is there anybody I can ask?"

"Why would you want to do that?" asked Mark.

"I mean, I want to know what I have to look forward to. Are we in England?" said Grey.

"Haha, you know, I don't think countries exist like that anymore. Best not to worry about all this just yet. It's a long sentence. You'll drive yourself crazy looking ahead all of the time," said Mark. "Trust me, Rainy, it's better to find the positives in the moment around here."

Grey bit his cheek angrily. The current moment was a white hallway. What life-affirming positives could he draw from that? He forced himself to take a deep breath, counting to ten before responding. "What's that word you keep using? Rainy?"

"Re-animated folks, Rainies," said Mark cheerfully. "Little modern colloquialism. It's what we call ourselves. What everybody calls us, really."

"Even outside?" Grey asked.

"I guess," Mark shrugged. "It's what the guards call us at least."

"I see. *Rainy*," said Grey, trying the word out for himself. "Are there many others? Rainies, I mean."

Mark shook his head. "Not a ton, no. It never really caught on, vitrification I mean. People started reading the fine print. They realised pretty quickly that you'd probably wake up dirty poor in an unrecognisable society that you couldn't possibly hope to contribute to with your outdated skills," Mark spread his arms wide, gesturing to their surroundings. "Not like us lucky bastards. We're the anomalies. Unskilled labour, baby."

Graham thought. "Did you say Labour and Maintenance?"

"Lifting and mopping, it should be," said Mark, guiding them round a corner. "Since that's mostly what we do. We're a good team. Just under two dozen of us. Keep MerryCom clean and polished for whatever nefarious business they get up to." He winked.

Grey wondered if MerryCom really needed the services of two dozen skill-less, expensively rebuilt bodies for this job, or if it was merely a place to put useless Rainies.

Mark and Grey approached two women wearing the same uniform as them and holding hands. Mark nodded, winking charmingly at the prettier of the two. She flushed a lovely red and smiled.

"That's Cherry," said Mark once they were out of earshot. "I've been working on that one for a while."

The moment was so reminiscent of walking home from the pub with friends that Grey found himself smiling. "Hands off, got it."

"Nah, I'm not worried," said Mark. "I don't think she's into pretty boys like you."

"Of course not," said Grey with a wry smile. "I'm ravishing. It's a lot to take in."

Mark let out that booming laugh once again. "Excellent. I thought you might have a sense of humour under all that doom and gloom,"

"And I'd probably have assumed she was gay. Isn't she with the woman she was holding hands with?" remarked Grey.

"Oh my god" Mark chuckled. "You grandad. You should know that humans abandoned the idea of defining sexuality a long time ago. It was really an awkward little blip in our timeline that people felt the need to do that. Love who you love, my friend,"

Grey paused for a second, before nodding with complete sense-making acceptance. They passed another set of guards who Mark nodded to before he pushed open a door and gestured for Grey to enter. "Hold onto your humour though, because this place will take a lot of other things away from you. Definitely your ego."

The room was predictably white. Grey thought back to the artist colonies promised in the orientation video with a sneer. Apparently MerryCom missed the memo. Two white benches lined adjacent walls. Three Rainies, if the slate uniforms could be believed, draped comfortably across them. At the back of the room was a round table with several chairs sitting next to a round shape inset into the wall. As Grey watched, a Rainy woman seated at the table reached into the opaque circle and pulled out a mug. The smell of coffee filled the room. Grey took in the scent with a rush of nostalgia. Suddenly he was in a much bigger room with its great windows overlooking the London cityscape-

"Roll call," called Mark and the Rainies turned their attention to Grey. "Everybody meet Grey. This is Troy," Mark gestured to a dark-haired man on one of the benches. "That's Matthias next to him. Across from him is Ishaan - watch out for him, he's got two left feet, I swear,"

"Why don't you just-" Ishaan said, making an obscene hand gesture in Mark's direction. "Nice to meet you, mate," he turned to Grey with a friendly smile.

"Hey," Grey nodded his greeting.

"And last but not least," said Mark, gesturing wildly to the woman at the table. "We have the saint herself! You know her, you love her, the one, the only-,"

"Mish," she interrupted. "I'm just Mish. Honestly, Mark, you missed your calling in entertainment," She clutched her mug with long fingers and rolled her almond shaped eyes at him. Her hair was a riot of black curls that framed her face and spilt over her shoulders. Looking at her now, Grey was surprised he hadn't noticed her sooner.

"There's always time, love," said Mark.

"Well, don't forget us little guys, then," said Mish. She sipped her coffee gingerly.

"I could never," said Mark. "Anyway, now you've met everybody. Welcome to the Labour and Maintenance team. We meet here every morning, 8am - don't be late - and we work until 8pm. Each workday is one full credited day towards your sentence."

"That's kind of them," said Grey.

"Yeah, it almost makes up for the food," said Matthias.

"The food isn't that terrible," said Mish. "Don't scare him."

Mark slapped Grey on the back. "Not Grey here. This one eats nails for breakfast,"

Mish raised one dark eyebrow in his direction and Grey found himself smiling.

"Good source of iron," he said. Mish smiled and it lit up her entire face. Grey had a sudden urge to hear her laugh. He had a feeling it was spectacular.

There was a knock at the door: one of the guards telling them to get a move on.

"It's about that time," Ishaan stretched as he stood. "Who wants to teach the newbie how to block out the trashers?"

"I will," said Mish with a slow smile, her eyes locked on Grey. "I don't want you lot ruining this one,"

*

'Blocking out the trashers' turned out to be a whimsical turn of phrase for a challenging job. After the group left the break room, Mish led him down another white hallway into an empty mess hall.

"We only do this after the Protos leave," she said.

"Protos?" asked Grey. He was trying not to get frustrated with his own ineptitude. He wished Mish could have seen him in his own time, back when he was capable. Impressive even.

"Prototypicals. People who are living their original lives. The opposite of us," said Mish. "MerryCom doesn't like too much interaction between mainstream society and our sub-society,"

"Why not?"

"I suspect there's some resentment on both ends, not that that's the company's official position. Don't quote me on it, but there's a good reason that Protos aren't worried about this slavery racket in their beautiful utopia. They hate us, Grey. We wrecked the planet, put their ancestors through hell and then we rock up and think we can just carry on after they've cleaned up the mess." Mish led him past the rows of tables to the back of the room.

"How do you know all of this? If they keep everybody so separate?" asked Grey.

Mish turned her dark eyes on Grey, who took the opportunity to study the planes of her face. "I'm pretty good at reading people," she said after a moment.

Grey looked away. He wasn't sure he was ready for Mish to read him yet. He wasn't sure how he would measure up in his grey uniform and absolute ignorance of the time he was living in.

"You see this circle on the floor?" she had crouched down and was pointing to a circular seam in the polished concrete. It was so thin that Grey would have assumed it was a vein in the stone, if he noticed it at all.

"Yes, I do," he said, crouching beside her.

"This is the trasher," she said. "You turn it like this," she webbed her fingers across it and twisted. "And it opens like that," The circle hissed slightly as it lifted, and a silver tube rose out of the floor. Higher and higher it climbed until it was well above Grey's head.

"What is it?" Grey asked once it stilled.

"It's a compactor," said Mish. "For trash."

"Lovely," said Grey. He put his hands on his hips and glared up at the top of the trasher. "I don't know why I assumed a society like this would have moved beyond trash."

"They tried," said Mish with a snort. She had piled her curls on the top of her head and secured them with an elastic. The effect was distractingly undone, intimate somehow, like she'd just rolled out of bed. "They got pretty close. After the climate wars they couldn't afford to waste anything, and society developed from there. These are mostly for composting foodstuffs."

"'Foodstuffs,'" Grey laughed.

"What?" asked Mish sharply.

"I've never heard anybody use that word."

"It's a great word," Mish shrugged. "Anyway, the trashers compact the waste and once a month we empty them," She led him to another hidden door in the wall that revealed a closet holding a stack of disks about the size of a hula hoop. She grabbed two, handing him one, and returned to the trasher. "This is the bag, just press that little red button - yeah just like that,"

The disk sprung open into a canvas bag shaped like the janitorial trash cans of his time. The bag floated about an inch above the concrete floor.

"Magic?" Grey raised an eyebrow.

"Magnets," Mish smiled again, and Grey felt it in his chest. "Don't get too excited. They float to protect the finish on the floors. They're still heavy as hell,"

Grey flexed his arms subtly. "I think I can handle it."

"We'll see about that, tough guy," said Mish. She opened a small door on the silver tube and reached in with both hands, extracting a black lump no larger than a Rubix cube. With an inexplicable grunt of effort, she dropped the cube into the canvas can. "Your turn."

Grey couldn't tell whether she was messing with him or not, but he didn't want to lose face. He approached the tube and glanced in. There was another cube sitting on a silver shelf deep inside. He reached in and wrapped his fingers around it. He pulled. Nothing happened. The cube barely shifted on the shelf. He reached in with both hands and successfully pulled it out, startled by the weight of it. He dropped the black block unceremoniously into the canvas where it clinked dully against the first cube like the heaviest choice from a bowling ball rack.

"What the?" Grey panted lightly. "That's got to weigh 20 kilos."

The corner of Mish's mouth rose in a crooked smile. "Each tube holds 30."

Grey ran a nervous hand through his hair. "How many tubes are there?"

"Ten."

*

After emptying the trashers, they had to drag the filled canvas bags down a flight of stairs to a hydroponic station where they were collected by a bleary-eyed Rainy who had clearly just woken.

"He'll process the blocks into nutrients for the hydroponic farms," Mish explained. "He's on the science track. He'll serve as much time as us, but he gets to take naps."

They collapsed the canvas disks and returned them to the storage closet before moving on to the floor. Mopping, at least, Grey was familiar with. It was humiliating to admit, but scrubbing the polished concrete was the only task Grey had felt competent in all day. He winced as his back ached, certain it would sting tomorrow, and he realised Mark was right about MerryCom's propensity to take away the ego.

The one bright spot was Mish. She had moved quickly from interesting to beautiful. He found himself admiring the grace she brought to the most menial jobs. She moved like a dancer, gliding smoothly between each task. Grey observed that she was strong, and he wondered if her physical prowess came from being part of the Labour and Maintenance crew or from her first life.

They broke for lunch and re-joined the others in the break room. Somebody had left a tray of sandwiches for them. Grey sat gingerly between Ishaan and Mark, back aching, and ate. The sandwiches were dry, but surprisingly satisfying after an afternoon of working. Grey chuckled as he realised that sandwiches had stood the test of time.

"What do we have next?" he asked the room when he'd finished eating.

"You finished the floor of the mess?" asked Mark.

"Yeah."

"Great work," Mark patted him on the shoulder. "Now we do the kitchens."

The kitchens went much faster with all of them working. They had the trashers emptied and the floors scrubbed in half the time it took him and Mish to finish the mess hall. As they tucked away the last of the canvas disks, Grey's Chroniker vibrated. He glanced down at the little projection that read '1c', stomach sinking. This was the next eleven years of his life. Backbreaking, boring, unskilled work.

"Look at that," said Mish, pulling him from his dark thoughts. She glanced at his Chroniker and leaned in closer to him. "The first one is the hardest, you'll see," Grey could count the honey-coloured flecks in her eyes.

He cleared his throat. "Maybe," he managed some sort of a smile and turned to walk away. A small, warm hand stopped him.

"We should celebrate," said Mish. "Seriously. Do you want to grab a drink tonight?"

"Sure," said Grey too quickly. "I mean, yeah. Let's do that."

"Great," Mish grinned at him and suddenly it was like he hadn't spent the day hauling impossibly heavy blocks and scrubbing floors.

"Great," he was staring at her. He realised it, but he couldn't make himself stop. He needed a cover. "Should we - ah, should we ask the others?"

"Let's not," said Mish, smiling back. "I think I want you to myself."

Grey couldn't have stopped smiling if he tried. Later, when he was escorted through the slightly less labyrinthine halls back to his room, Mark narrowed his eyes at Grey.

"Why do you look like somebody gifted you their credits?"

"No reason," said Grey. "Can people do that?"

Mark shrugged. "They can. Not sure why anybody would waste them on your useless mug, though," Mark shoved Grey's shoulder and he stumbled forward with a laugh. Something warm was spreading in his chest. Not even the armoured guards could have intimidated him at that moment.

It was almost like having a friend.

SEVEN

If there was one invention in the course of human existence that couldn't be improved upon (at least, not by very much), Grey was certain it was the shower. A marvel of human ingenuity. Man's mastery of the elements to provide the ultimate comforting convenience.

Back in his room, glaring at the opaque tube, he quickly realised that the people of the 23rd century didn't share his sentiment. The process of opening the tube was as unintuitive and complicated as everything else in the time period. He paced all fifteen steps of his room looking for instructions.

He tried to open the tube and found there were no hinges. The tube didn't lift or slide from side to side. It didn't twist or collapse. Finally, he kicked it. It remained impenetrable, taunting him from its place in the corner and Grey felt a rising panic. He was living in a time where the most basic of life's skills eluded him. The reality of his own incompetence nearly made him ill. He couldn't even clean himself. Reduced to the proficiency of a toddler, Grey contemplated running at the tube and smashing it with his head. He figured either the tube or his skull would crack and either option was better than standing around, stupid and sweaty.

Then he saw it.

The ever so slightly iridescent disk imprinted on the tube. He splayed his fingers across it and twisted, much the way Mish had opened the trashers, and a man-sized doorway slid open. Grey eyed it for a moment, imagining himself pulverised into a little block for Sleepy Steve in hydroponics to feed his hydrangeas.

In the end, the promise of cleanliness won over his anxiety. Grey eased himself into the tube, which slid shut behind him. There were three disks inside, helpfully labelled: 1,2, and 3. Grey spun the first disk and a shower of warm water cascaded from the ceiling. He leaned his head back with a happy sigh. It was heaven, with the steam rising in sweet-smelling spirals and the warm water on his back rinsing away the day of labour. The tube cast a soft light from somewhere deep within its walls, giving the entire experience a dreamlike quality.

When he rotated the second disk the water quality changed. It became thicker, the sweet smell stronger. Grey ran a hand over his head, and it came back filled with bubbles. He scrubbed and lathered himself, marvelling at the luxurious, viscous texture. The water shifted again, the spray rinsing him clean in seconds before stopping with sudden precision.

Grey sighed, feeling content for the first time since his reanimation. It was amazing what a good shower could do. Aside from some general muscle soreness from exertion, Grey felt great. The ache in his shoulder had faded and even the scar was disappearing. And he had to admit that his vision *had* improved. He wondered what else they had done to him in that storage locker.

He twisted the third disk, certain it would open the tube, and was surprised when it released a burst of warm air that dried him instantly. Apparently, a waste-free society had little use for towels. He felt a pang of sadness remembering his royal blue 850gsm bath towels at home.

Once he stepped out of the tube, clothing became a more immediate issue. The grey shirt and trousers seemed to have disappeared during his shower. Buoyed by his shower success, Grey searched the room for more iridescent disks. He found one quickly with a better sense of what he was looking for this time and spun it. A rack of clothing slid out of the wall, though 'rack' was far too generous of a word. On it was the missing clothing, as well as two identical sets in black and white. Grey pondered for a moment, then pulled on the black outfit, wishing he had more than the tiny shaving mirror above the sink to check his appearance.

"Visitor," said the room as he finished dressing. "Visitor,"

"Thank you," said Grey, unsure if he was supposed to but not wanting to offend his room. He found the door disk and spun it, swallowing his adrenaline as the door slid open and Mish poked her head in.

"About ready?" she asked, and her voice was more comforting than a dozen tube showers. She looked relaxed in black jeans and a white t-shirt that glowed against her skin. She had taken her hair down and the curls frothed around her face.

Grey glanced down at his own black ensemble. "I didn't realise we could mix and match," He was thinking of his clothes back home, longing for his pristine wardrobe.

Mish's nose crinkled when she laughed, a bell-like sound that made Grey smile. "Nobody cares what we wear. We're basically alone after the facility closes anyway. Unless you count the guards, which most of us don't." She didn't seem bothered by the lack of attention.

"That's awfully trusting of them," said Grey. He wiped his hands discreetly on his trousers. "Leaving a bunch of assets alone overnight,"

"One day blocking out the trashers and he thinks he's an asset," Mish said to the room. She crossed her arms with a smile and leaned against his doorway.

"I am surprisingly competent, I know," said Grey.

"You are surprisingly *slow*," Mish wrinkled her nose at him. "Let's get a move on."

Grey's nerves faded as Mish led him through the facility, nodding respectfully at every guard they passed. Grey would have found their armed presence unsettling, but Mish distracted him expertly. She was incredibly easy to talk to, quick witted with a biting sense of humour. He walked her through his experience with the shower tube, exaggerating the details and poking fun at his incompetence. Anything to hear her laugh again. It was quickly becoming his favourite sound.

"In many ways the shower reminded me of this art exhibit I loved, the Kusama Mirror Rooms. They were in London for a while. You'd step into a small room covered in mirrors, pools of water and glowing lights, and it would leave you with a sense of infinite space, of calm," said Grey.

"I don't think I saw that one," Mish replied.

"The last time I went, they let two groups in at a time for a three-minute interval, and it was me and a couple who were clearly on their first date. And they were both so insecure, that neither could stay quiet and experience the art. They awkwardly tried to take a selfie together, but it came out dark, so they ended up just taking photos of the room, and he said this line about how he'd got the tickets through his company's scheme, something cringe about the perks of dating an accountant… anyway I swore I'd always be careful how much I waffle on in dates after that."

"So, this is a date?" asked Mish

Grey went red. "Oh I didn't mean to say that, it's just-"

"I'm kidding, it's a date, a friend date. I asked you on a friend date," Mish laughed awkwardly.

She led him up two flights of stairs and through a set of double doors to a makeshift canteen. It was a large (predictably) white room scattered with round tables and chairs where dozens of Rainies were laughing and drinking together. There was a buffet to the right where a line of Rainies were serving themselves dinner. The source-less light was soft and dim and unfamiliar music poured from invisible speakers. The overall effect was that of a speakeasy or some secret underground bunker.

"How does this work?" he asked as Mish guided them to the buffet line. "Do they add it to our bill, or-?"

Mish looked at him like he had suddenly sprouted a second head. "They have to feed us, Grey. Operational costs."

"Oh. That's good," Grey said.

Mish placed two plates on the buffet counter for them. "Food isn't commoditised here the way it was back in our time. Not for money anyway. Everybody needs to eat, so everybody is fed."

Grey squinted at her. "Are you telling me we solved world hunger?"

"Turns out it was less of a shortage and more of a distribution problem," said Mish, serving herself a pile of mashed potatoes. Grey followed suit and loaded his plate, relieved to find that food hadn't changed much in two hundred years.

But maybe that was a result of MerryCom 'easing our transitions', Grey thought uneasily.

"What are you drinking and is it wine, beer, or whiskey?" Mish asked as they reached the end of the buffet.

"We get alcohol?" Grey asked, eyeing the glass bottles on the shelves behind the buffet. They were all the same shape and size but labelled with generic black lettering. Sure enough, there were only three options.

"Alcohol is a huge part of human culture as a whole," said Mish. She pulled a 'Beer' bottle from the wall and placed it on her tray. "It's extra calories and it keeps morale up, so we get one drink a day."

Who was Grey to argue with 23rd century science? He grabbed a bottle labelled 'Whiskey' and followed Mish to a table.

"You said 'our time'," said Grey, setting his tray down across the table from Mish. "What makes you so sure we came from the same time?"

"The slang gives it away,"

"Really?" Grey raised an eyebrow.

"Oh yeah, I'm telling you, when Mark gets going I can't understand a bloody thing he's saying," she said, cracking open her beer and taking a deep swig. "You'd be surprised how much language relies on context,"

"I never thought of that," Grey admitted. "Can I ask when you were born? If it's not too impolite-,"

"Of course you can," said Mish with a smile. "I was born in 2028 and vitrified in 2062. You?"

"Born in 1988 and vitrified in 2021," he said, opening his bottle of whiskey, which fizzed suspiciously.

"Just missed me," Mish's eyes were dark and liquid in the dim light when she looked at him.

"I guess so," Grey found himself smiling back. He smiled a lot around her, he noticed. "I think you're older than me, technically speaking."

"Or I'm 40 years younger. What is age, really?" Mish laughed.

"Cheers," Grey agreed, clinking her bottle with his own. "So how did you manage to get yourself reanimated first?"

"They work backwards," said Mish. "I mean, they screen for usefulness, of course. People with comorbidities or major physical imperfections have to wait a little longer to be redeployed, which is horrible, of course. But they mostly go by time period. The vitrification process improved a lot over the years. Older bodies are harder to reanimate, I guess, less upgrades!"

"We must be on the tail end then. It was a cutting-edge process back in my day."

"They were saving the best for last. And then they got so distracted with me that they forgot you for an extra three years," Mish winked.

"Hilarious," Grey deadpanned. "I bet they were so busy whipping you into shape they didn't have any resources left for me."

Mish nodded, gravely. "I'm a terror, that's for sure."

"I don't believe that for a second," said Grey. "You strike me as the Florence Nightingale type."

Mish snorted into her plate. "Careful, you're ageing us both with that reference."

"What is age, really?" Grey asked, crinkling his nose back at her. "So, what made you do it?"

"Vitrify?" asked Mish. "Curiosity, mostly. I think I wanted to see how much people could change when enough time went by."

Grey smiled at that. "What did you do? Back in your first life."

"I was a social worker," Mish took another swig of her beer. "For children and families. I assisted with foster placements, but my main focus was reuniting siblings and families within the system."

Grey let out a low whistle. "That's - that's really amazing, Mish. Wow,"

She shrugged, her cheeks colouring, and the movement might have read as false humility on anybody else. On her it was perfect.

"It was amazing, sometimes, yeah," she said. She was looking at him, but he could tell she was seeing something from her past. Her eyes had a dreamy, unfocused quality and her smile slipped just a little. "It was great when we managed to reconnect them, you know? Like, I remember, we found this boy's sister once who'd been missing in the system for three years. Then we found them a placement together and it was just-," she shook her head and looked away, lost in her thoughts. "That's what I wanted every day. Those small miracles, right? Making the world easier where I could,"

She looked like a work of art in the soft lighting, lost in wistful memory. A creature of air and stone that he managed to find in this strange place. She caught his eye and winked, a slow smile growing across her face. "I know it's cheesy saying it out loud."

Grey shook his head. "No. It's really not."

There was a strange feeling building in his chest. A strange realisation that this was the most honest conversation he had ever had with a woman. A sudden understanding that, for all his money and prowess, he had never aspired to even a crumb of Mish's altruism. That it had never occurred to him to alter the world around him for the better. He was too busy working the system to consider changing it and, in that moment, stripped of his worldly assets, he didn't deserve to be sitting at her table, making her laugh, stealing bites of her potatoes.

"A social worker, huh?" said Grey. He needed the conversation to change. He was feeling an unsettling lack of control that made his hands shake. "How did you end up here, then? Was it part of the pension plan?"

Mish snorted. "Hardly. It was part of an inheritance I got from my uncle. Vitrification was taking off, so he set the whole thing up for me."

"Wow," said Grey.

"Yeah. He knew I could never afford it on my salary," she said. "He was always trying to get me to quit my job and work for him."

"But you wouldn't?"

"I loved it," Mish smiled again. "I want to do something similar when I get out of here. I bet it'll be more of the good and less of the bad."

"If they have fosters at all," said Grey. Mish's face fell and he wanted to kick himself. It was an old habit, cutting people down when they got too close. How many of his dates ended just like this? What was it about passionate people that intimidated him?

Mish recovered quickly. Her positivity was unflappable. "Maybe they don't have jobs at all,"

Grey smiled his apology, knowing that he was forgiven when she smiled back. "What will you do in that case?"

"Cook," she said without a moment's hesitation. "I'll cook amazing food all day long."

"Save some for me."

"What about you?" she asked.

"Me?"

"What were you like, back in the day?" Mish pushed her tray to the side and rested her chin in her hands.

In his old life, it would have been an easy question. Grey was all about the elevator pitch. He could compartmentalise and polish up his life into the prettiest little package. *I am successful. I am in control.* But he couldn't bring himself to be like that with Mish. He could sense that his usual lines wouldn't work on her. She was too comfortable in her skin to respond to his games, and he was sure she would know if he was pretending. And he didn't want to pretend. There was something warm and safe between them that Grey felt he needed to protect,

"I, er - I worked in corporate strategy," that seemed a safe place to start.

Mish looked at him expectantly.

"It wasn't a passion or anything," he said finally. "Just something to do, I guess."

"I imagine few people consider corporate strategy particularly exhilarating," said Mish. "What brought you to it?"

He swallowed a mouthful of whiskey, savouring the burn to buy him some time. His hands were shaking again. They were on dangerous ground and Mish didn't even realise it. She blinked at him innocuously, oblivious to his racing heart.

"My dad was kind of...strict, a driver..." it was like the words had been exorcised from him, a dam breaking somewhere inside of him. "He had these- I don't know- these ideas about how to be successful and I just... went along with them."

Mish's gaze didn't waiver from his face. "That sounds like a lot of pressure."

"It could be, yeah," Grey said, as if he hadn't thrived under his father's guidance. As if he hadn't wanted the money or the power or the apartment. "I don't - it's hard to remember sometimes. There are gaps."

This, at least, was true. In searching his memories Grey quickly realised there was very little substance there. He had work and lonely nights in his apartment, punctuation by the occasional fight with his father or hook up with Sally. He couldn't tell Mish that. Sweet Mish who dedicated her life to reuniting lost children and dreamed of cooking all day long.

Hollow.

"It's probably revival fog," said Mish, saving him from his own self-hatred. "Older bodies are harder to reanimate. Sometimes it takes a while for the mind to catch up,"

"Maybe," Grey finished the rest of his whiskey in one gulp. It was definitely weaker than he was used to.

"No pressure," Mish's mouth quirked up once more. "We've got plenty of time,"

"Yeah," said Grey, warmth blooming in his chest. *We.*

"What made you decide to vitrify?" she asked, her tone switching back to playful. "Overwhelming fear of death?"

"Fear of death?"

"Of course. That's what ultimately did it for me. Well, that and the rich uncle."

Grey was surprised how readily she admitted it without a trace of discomfort or shame. "You're afraid of dying?"

"Aren't you?"

He considered for a moment, about to deny it, but then he remembered the smell of smoke and the screams of the dying. The way the mud had pulled at his feet as if the ground was trying to reclaim him. "I - I actually think I am," he laughed but it was a dark, humourless sound. "I don't think I've ever admitted that, even to myself."

Mish studied him for a moment, eyes full of amusement. "Not ever?"

Grey shook his head. "Not openly, no. I like...," he paused, unsure how to proceed and embarrassed at how readily he was sharing the information.

"Control?" she finished for him. "You seem like you've got some type A in there for sure."

"Something like that," Grey laughed for real this time. "You really are observant, aren't you?"

"Hazard of the occupation," she said. "You'll learn to appreciate it."

Grey smiled again, stacking their trays together and pushing them to the side of the table.

"I think already do."

EIGHT

Grey learned that time moved steadily when his days were filled with activity. The first few weeks were an overwhelming blur, punctuated here and there with benign milestones; finding his own way to the canteen, reprogramming the canvasses when one of the magnets broke, learning which guards would harass him for a uniform violation or coming too close to oversleeping, realising that the closet in his room had a laundry function. Each night he collapsed into bed, body aching and completely tired in a way he was pretty sure he had never been in his first life. And before he knew it, difficult weeks slipped seamlessly into months.

He fell into a steady routine. Morning, breakfast with Mark, work, dinner with Mish, shower, and sleep. He had become as close a friend to Mark and Mish as anyone from his first life. There was a comfort in knowing exactly what each day would bring. The Labour and Maintenance chores were done on a rotating schedule, changing only in the case of an emergency. 'Emergency' in this case meant minor equipment breakdown or the spilling of a Proto's lunch in the cafeteria. Those few deviations were simply a novel break in the day, taken in stride. Overall, the rigour appealed to Grey's desire for control.

That wasn't to say Grey couldn't appreciate spontaneity. Sometimes, after working hours, he would go on long, ambling walks with Mark. He liked listening to Mark philosophise about the nuts and bolts of being human in his unique, affable way. He appreciated the opportunity to map out the Ark. Mark had a wonderful way of finding something to appreciate in every moment. Blocking out the trashers was a free workout, the simple food at the canteen reminded him of camping when he was a child, verbally sparring with the guards kept his wit sharp; Mark could always find the silver lining.

And there was Mish. Beautiful, brilliant, biting Mish. He was embarrassingly hooked on the woman. Past Grey would have scoffed if he could see him now. Before comfortable exhaustion claimed him at night, Grey lay in bed mulling over their interactions like a schoolboy. *She touched my shoulder when she said good morning. That must mean she likes me.* It was bordering on pathetic, he thought, but he couldn't bring himself to feel ashamed. It was more than an attraction. Grey had plenty of experience wanting women - his relationship with Sally came to mind - but this was something different. Something pure. He admired her, the way her mind worked, her unconscious altruism. It was enough to be around her in any capacity. Her presence made his world easier. But he worried that it was a one-sided benefit, and he was desperate to make himself as indispensable to her as she was becoming to him.

With all of the confusion around birthdays versus rebirth days, it was much easier to celebrate Chroniker milestones. Rainies didn't mind so much, it seemed, being reminded of their Chroniker credit score when the excuse for a party came with it. Mark mentioned as much on one of their walks and Grey filed the information away, putting his scheming brain to use trying to figure out a way to plan something for Mish. He imagined a celebration, Mish glowing with excitement, and enough alcohol and goodwill to create an atmosphere where anything could happen. He planned things he would say, tripping over his own feelings and wondering how he ever thought he was good at approaching women. There was no Grouchos, no secret drinks in darkened corners, no fancy car or job to impress her with. He was, in some ways, at a loss without his usual tricks.

Luck came in the form of Mish's Chroniker. It announced her three-year milestone with a projected miniature confetti cannon while they were seeding new flower beds on the main MerryCom campus. Grey jumped at the cannon sound and froze for a mortifying couple of seconds while his mind caught up to the reality that he was safe at MerryCom smelling the rich soil and flowers in their beds, and not the blood and muck of the battlefield.

When he finally blinked away the memory of smoke and ash from his eyes, Mish was watching him worriedly. He suspected Mark had clued her in to his previous experience, though she was kind enough not to ask and he was kind enough not to tell her. The occasional nightmares were bad enough without rehashing them in the bright light of midday, so he fixed a smile on his face to comfort her.

"Three years!" Mark hollered from his place at the other side of the lawn. He waved his thickly gloved hands in the air and danced them around. That got the rest of the guys hooting and hollering while Mish blushed at the attention.

"That's enough," shouted the guard posted at the entrance to the MerryCom facility. The Rainies stopped, turning their attention back to the work at hand. Grey glared at the black uniform and helmet that covered the guard's eyes. The guards would always be unsettling to him. Not for the first time, he wondered if they were human at all. Sometimes he imagined them melting into metallic puddles Terminator-style.

Mish met Grey's eyes over the flower bush they were wrestling into the ground. "You're coming tonight, right?"

Grey didn't know where they were going, but he nodded immediately. He knew that he would willingly clean the trashers every day for a year if it meant he could spend every day with her.

*

"You got a plan?" Mark asked Grey. He smiled at a guard as they passed on their way to the canteen, his face the picture of innocence.

"Why would I need a plan?" asked Grey, keeping his voice low and trying not to move his mouth too much.

"For the drinks," Mark looked incredulous. "I'm looking for backup here, man. I can't always be the mastermind."

"Backup? This was your idea. You said it was no big deal! 'Oi, Grey, come with me to get drinks for the party',"

"Don't say the word that begins with 'p' and ends in 'arty'," said Mark, his eyes darting around the crowded hall. It was after the end of the last shift, and Rainies and guards were milling about on their way to their rooms or to a late dinner. "And don't look at me like that."

Grey's expression remained unchanged. "What are we doing here?"

Mark ducked his head, looking for all the world like he was making a bad impression of a criminal in an old-timey movie. "Okay, listen. I wouldn't say what we're doing is against policy, but it's definitely frowned upon."

"Mark," Grey kept his voice even. "Please tell me you didn't bring me along to help you steal alcohol from the canteen."

"I wouldn't say it's stealing, exactly. We're just getting an advance on our alcohol ration," said Mark.

"I'm not sure it matters whether *you would say it's stealing*," Grey hissed.

Mark rolled his eyes. "Okay, okay, I've got a plan. Honestly, man, I just wanted you to feel included in the decision-making process."

"Thanks for that," said Grey flatly. "I really feel like one of the guys,"

"You know, it's your earnest disposition and overall optimism that drew me to you in the first place," said Mark.

Grey snorted. "I bet,"

"Now you say something nice about me," said Mark, pushing open the doors to the breezeway.

"You conned me into larceny. Why would I say something nice about you?"

"Because this is our first fight and therefore our first makeup," said Mark.

"You're living in a different world," said Grey, shaking his head.

"Thank you," Mark smiled gleefully. "Now seriously, we need a plan,"

"What happens if we get caught?" asked Grey.

"No point worrying ourselves with that," said Mark.

Grey chewed on the inside of his cheek, trying his hardest not to look away when they passed a group of guards. What was it about trying to avoid suspicion that made his every move feel suspicious? "Feels like something we should consider,"

"All there is is this moment, worrying about the rest is useless because it hasn't happened yet," said Mark. "We're going to take this one step at a time and we're not going to overthink it, alright?"

Grey wasn't sure he was capable of not overthinking, but he nodded anyway, refreshed by Mark's candid logic. "Whatever you say," They were approaching the doors to the canteen. Grey could hear the chatter on the other side. He wiped his palms on his jeans and followed Mark through the doorway.

"Don't worry, man," said Mark under his breath. "I figured out our plan," His face split into a grin.

The "plan" ended up being more of a stroke of luck than a calculation on their part. That stroke of luck came in the form of Cherry being scheduled to work the buffet line. Mark's entire disposition changed when he saw her. His spine straightened and his anxious steps smoothed as he breezed over and began charming her silly. Which left Grey to sneak around the back and shove bottles into the deep pockets of his jeans, down his shirt, anywhere he could hide them.

They slouched out of the canteen with pockets full of alcohol and a promise that Cherry would swing by after her shift. They were the picture of innocence - if innocence involved waddling down the hall to prevent stolen alcohol bottles from clinking together in their pockets. Grey's heart was pounding so loudly he was sure it would cover the sounds of any contraband anyway. But it wasn't unpleasant. It was a kind of childhood thrill, like building a fort or sneaking chocolate into bed. He was giddy, high on his own arrogance. The risk was stressful, but well worth the feeling of camaraderie. By the time they got to Mish's room he thought he might have been floating.

Mish threw her arms around Grey's neck when she saw him. Grey winced at the loud *clink* of the bottles in his pockets, but accepted the embrace gratefully, pulling her to him. He could feel the skin of her cheek against his neck and the warmth of her breath. The moment was shockingly intimate and over far too soon. Her eyes were bright, and her cheeks flushed, he noticed as she broke from him and hugged Mark equally as sloppily.

"Are you drunk already?" asked Mark, catching her with one arm.

Mish wrinkled her nose and giggled like a naughty child. "Maybe," She dragged them into the room and shut the door behind them. Ishaan and Troy were perched on the bed, drinks in hand.

"Excuse me? How?" Mark was incredulous. He pulled bottles out of his pockets and slammed them on the desk. "Grey and I went James Bond down there to get you alcohol."

"It's true," said Grey. "There were wires and lasers and everything."

"We risked life and limb," Mark continued.

"Who is James Bond?" asked Matthias. Mark looked murderous.

"Troy and Ishaan tucked some into a canvas when we were doing the trashers in there," Mish turned to Ishaan with a conspiratorial grin and Grey felt the sting of something dangerously close to jealousy.

"Fucking brilliant," Mark ran a hand over his face. "Why didn't we think of that?"

"Lack of imagination," Grey said, trying to keep the dejection out of his voice.

"That'll do it," Mark grabbed a whiskey and tossed it to Grey and then opened one for himself. "Where is part two of the dream team?"

"He's bringing food," said Matthias. "He's got a hook up at the buffet,"

"Of course he does," Mark grumbled.

"Life and limb, eh?" said Mish in Grey's ear. She had piled her hair on the top of her head in some sort of elaborate knot with delicate stray wisps framing her face. Her eyes were bright with liquor and she was beautifully flushed. He wanted to reach out and tuck the escaped hair behind her ear, to run his thumb across her cheek. He downed half of his whiskey instead.

"Absolutely," he said with a little cough as the alcohol burned his throat. "You're lucky I made it in one piece,"

"Thank goodness," she bumped her shoulder against his with a wink. "I definitely want you in one piece."

The room got louder and warmer as the night went on and they worked their way through both Troy and Mark's pilfered bottles. There was just enough room for everybody to sit without touching, but rather than being uncomfortable the room took on an atmosphere similar to a childhood sleepover. The noise swelled and built until somebody had the instinct to shush the rest of the group, lest an overeager guard make their way into the dorms. They played drinking games. Some Grey was familiar with, others he stumbled through good-naturedly. He took his losses, drinking until the room went fuzzy around the edges, then retreating to a spot on the bed where he could watch the others.

At some point Cherry appeared at the door and pulled Mark away from his lecture on the finer points of the Bond films to Matthias, who came from a time so far removed that he didn't entirely understand what a film was. Grey laughed at Matthias's sigh of relief when Cherry pulled Mark out of the room.

"What are you giggling about?" Mish asked, sitting next to him. Close enough that he could feel the heat of her but far enough away that they weren't touching. He thought about scooting closer. If this had been the old days he would have come up with a line - something about the air conditioning, or her not being dressed appropriately for the weather - and pulled her into his lap. Now he couldn't imagine commenting on her clothing and the idea of using a line on her (and her inevitable mocking after) was mortifying.

"I don't giggle," he said, tongue thick in his mouth. "I'm a man. We grunt to show approval," He wasn't slurring- yet- but his speech was slow and stumbling.

"Sure, right. My mistake," Mish rolled her eyes with a laugh.

There was a shout from the desk where Troy and Ishaan were playing a complicated drinking game that involved digital dice and a shot glass. Ishaan finished his bottle with an amiable shake of his head and reached for the holographically-projecting dice. Grey tried to follow the gameplay, hoping to pick up on the rules, but he couldn't keep up.

Mish leaned against the wall, pulling her knees up to her chest and resting her chin on them. She tilted her head and stared at him, a long beat where Grey could feel the heat rising in his chest, but he couldn't look away. After a while, she smiled.

"What?" he asked, feeling his own smile stretch across his face.

"What were you thinking about?" she asked.

Grey's ears felt uncomfortably warm. Was he blushing? "Just now?"

"Mmhmm," Mish nodded.

"Er, well - a lot of things, I guess," said Grey. "Laughing at Mark talking Matthias's ear off, and then how strange it is that Matthias is so much younger than us - technically speaking - but he's also years ahead of us, and then imagining the future. What I'll do when I get out of here. Where I want to go, what I think the world is going to be like," he shrugged

"That's a lot," said Mish softly. "Do you always spend your time at parties thinking about the future?"

"Not always," said Grey. He leaned closer, close enough to smell her shampoo and the wine on her breath. "Sometimes I get tipsy and sit on pretty girl's beds and *then* I think about the future."

"Seems like maybe you should try focusing on the pretty girl," Mish's voice was husky and soft. "And her bed."

Grey's heart was pounding in his ears. He couldn't stop staring at her lips - he wanted to kiss her - needed to touch her or he was going to-

"We're going to head out," Ishaan said, breaking the tension. Grey was seized with the urge to throttle him for the interruption. He clenched his nails into his palm instead. "Troy is done for. Are you coming, Grey?"

"No," Grey said, his eyes still locked with Mish. "No, I'm going to help clean up."

"Sure, yeah," Ishaan said, with a knowing smile. "Congrats again, Mish."

"Thanks, yeah," she said, smiling up at him. "Get home safe."

"Don't worry about us," Matthias called, attempting to sling one of Troy's arms over his shoulder. "This guy's the one who's going to be hurting."

Ishaan ducked under Troy's other arm and helped Matthias guide him out the door. Grey winced, not envying Troy for his inevitable hangover in the morning. They hauled him into the hallway, Ishaan grinning at Grey over his shoulder as the door slid shut.

And then they were alone.

The walls seemed to shrink in until the room felt absolutely miniscule. The reality of the space, Mish's space, was everywhere. He could smell her, could reach her soft skin inches away, if he could only make himself *move*. The air was heavy, charged with tension. Grey didn't need to look at Mish to feel her shifting beside him, the way she was looking everywhere but at him. Did she want him to leave? What if he reached for her and she recoiled? How would they feel after?

Her hand was in his. Grey didn't know which of them had reached for the other, but her skin was achingly soft and warm against his. Mish was looking at him with those wide, searching eyes, her cheeks flushed, her chest rising and falling.

He reached out a hand and brushed her hair behind her ear the way he'd always imagined doing. Her hair was like liquid silk in his hand, and she leaned into his palm. He stroked his thumb across her cheekbone and her eyes fluttered shut. Maybe it was the alcohol taking the edge off, but his mind was suddenly, blessedly quiet.

And then his hands were in her hair and he was kissing her, and it was better than every time he had imagined it. The reality of her - her hands on his shirt and then on his skin as she pulled it off of him and the realisation that he wasn't alone in wanting. He was drunk on alcohol and her hands on him and there was only that moment - Mish's lips against his, her skin against his skin, her moans in his ear - and the wave building in both of them as they came together. Building and breaking, elemental and primitive, a stolen moment in a space outside of time.

*

"I really was going to help you clean up," said Grey afterwards. He kissed Mish's forehead, smiling when she curled into him, resting her head on his chest, and threading her legs with his.

"Were you?" she asked. "I thought it was just a great line."

"Cleanliness gets you going, huh?"

"Of course. Why do you think I'm in Labour and Maintenance?" she said.

"Naughty," Grey chided. "I'll have to keep an eye on you when Ishaan is doing the floors."

She looked up at him with a wicked grin. "I knew you were jealous."

"Definitely not," Grey said.

She narrowed her eyes at him. "Liar."

Grey grinned at her, kissing her nose, her cheek, her lips. Honestly, vitrification had been worth it to get to that moment. In Mish's bed, with her collapsed and boneless in his arms, her eyes still bright with exertion.

"You're different," she said after a while, her voice soft with sleep.

"What do you mean?" he asked. He couldn't stop himself from touching her. He ran his fingers up and down her arm, marvelling at the petal softness.

"Happier," she said.

"Well, yeah," he snorted.

"Not because of that," she slapped his chest reprovingly. "I've noticed it for a while. When you first reanimated you were so withdrawn. Checking your Chroniker every couple of minutes. But now you seem, I don't know…content?"

Grey considered that. "I am," he said. And it was true. The months of labour had strengthened his body and his mind was alert and adaptable from constantly adjusting to his new timeline. He liked having a routine, knowing that he would wake up and see Mish in the morning and that they could go to work together. Knowing that they could have years filled with night-time conversations just like this. "I can't believe it, but I am."

"Yeah?"

"I know I should probably feel angry or tricked by MerryCom, but I don't," he said. It was a moment of rare honesty, fragile and new. "And I know I'm supposed to miss my old life, but I've realised that there wasn't much life to miss."

Mish's gaze was soft, and she tangled her fingers in his. "What was it like?"

He pushed her hair away from her forehead. Here, in the darkness of her room, drunk enough to be brave, he could finally put to words the thoughts that had consumed him for months.

"I wasn't a happy person back then," Grey said, his voice soft in the darkness. "I knew I was missing something, but I didn't know what. So, I went looking in all of the wrong places. I made money and when that didn't make me happy, I spent money. And then I made more money. I was always scheming, trying to figure out the next step. I didn't just want to succeed. I wanted to beat the game, you know? That's how I got into vitrification. I think I thought that I could 'beat death' and then I wouldn't be so scared all the time."

"Oh, Grey," said Mish. There was something soft in her voice, not pity, but something sweet and comforting.

"I was obsessed, I swear. It was all I thought about. But then, after I set up the whole process, the fear came back," Grey shook his head. "I needed a plan for when I reanimated: how I was going to live the life I was used to in the future. When vitrification hit the market, they passed legislation saying that we couldn't keep our assets post-mortem."

"I remember that," said Mish. "They had that in my time too. They didn't want people hoarding more wealth than they were already. It was bad for the economy taking all of that money out of circulation."

"Well, I was distressed," said Grey. "I worked hard to control every aspect of my life and I was being told I couldn't do the same in death."

"What did you do?" she asked, her thumb tracing little circles over his palm.

"It was so stupid," Grey laughed lightly. "My financial advisor and I thought we were so clever. We put my money into cryptocurrency - did you have crypto?"

"Yeah, of course."

"Well, we set up a seed password so I could access the account after reanimation. All I had to do was remember the password and I would have my money," Grey's eyes were growing heavy with sleep. "We didn't plan for the internet changing over the course of hundreds of years."

"Slight miscalculation," said Mish with her usual wry humour. "It was a good plan all the same."

"I don't know what we were thinking. We were so certain that Arcanum was the answer to everything. When I woke up here, I asked a counsellor to help me access it, but she laughed at me. I bet it collapsed after I vitrified."

Mish stiffened, her thumb stilling in his palm. "Arcanum?"

"Yeah," Grey yawned. "It was the hot new crypto at the time. Only the best for me." Sleep was pulling at him with tantalising fingers. He was exceedingly comfortable, drifting off with Mish rumpled and sleepy in his arms.

"Grey?" she whispered. "You don't remember the password, do you?"

"I don't know," he said, his tongue thick in his mouth. "I can't - maybe when I sober up. Why do you ask?"

She was quiet for a long time, nuzzling closer as Grey's breathing became deep and even. "It's nothing," she said so softly that Grey wasn't sure he had heard her at all.

NINE

The year was 2059.

It was a day like any other. Mish woke minutes before her alarm began screaming that it was time to start the day. It was another misty London morning and the shock of the cold floor against her bare feet did more to wake her than tea she brewed. She finished her tea standing at the kitchen counter, her eyes fixated on her calendar, wondering why he wanted to see her today. Wondering if he would show up at all. Oftentimes he didn't.

She abandoned her empty cup in the sink with a sigh. There was no point worrying about it. He would be there, or he wouldn't. Either way she had a job to do.

She showered and dressed warmly - it was going to be a long day, and nothing dampened her mood faster than a chill. Her satchel slung over her shoulder as she made her way to the tube. With its new retrofit, it had her to work in a matter of minutes.

The day flew by in a flurry of paperwork and phone calls. Mish had found placement for the Gutierrez siblings, a sweet trio of girls whose mother passed leaving them with no living relatives. The youngest found placement as quickly as most cherubic eight-year-old children did. The older two presented a problem, particularly the eldest. At twelve, she was at an age that fosters hesitated to take on. The middle sister might have fared better were it not for her anger at being separated from her siblings. Finding a home with the willingness and resources to take on the girls had taken her the better part of a month, but she had done it at last. After a couple of hours filling out forms and packing bags, the girls were tearfully reunited that afternoon, safely ensconced with a couple of empty nesters in a lovely district.

Mish left the siblings feeling a warm ache somewhere deep in her chest. She couldn't guarantee them an easy life, nothing as certain as that, but she could give them each other and make it a little easier going forward. She sighed, content for a moment before steeling herself for her next work task. The widow, Shelly Baker needed eldercare assistance, though she was a few years shy of the 75-year marker that would guarantee her placement at no cost. But Mish had a plan. Mish nearly always had a plan.

In spite of - or perhaps, because of - her busy day, the rest of the afternoon blew past. Mish sat at her desk long after the reasonable end of her shift, an uneasy knot settling in the pit of her stomach. Eventually, she gathered her things, knowing that she couldn't put it off any longer or she would be late. It was time for her meeting.

When she arrived, Henry Taylor was waiting outside the coffee shop, packed into a worn parka that looked like it was held together by thread and good intentions. Mish eyed him warily as she approached. His eyes were clear and bright, the same brown so dark that it might have been black as her own, and he had put on some weight. Mish was glad of that. She often worried that he wasn't feeding himself.

"Hi, Pumpkin," he smiled and pulled her into a cigarette-scented hug. Mish returned the embrace, closing her eyes for a moment, pretending she was little again.

"Hi, dad."

He pulled away, holding her at arm's length and taking stock. "Well, aren't you lovely,"

"You're biased," she quipped, pulling open the door and ushering him inside.

They ordered and claimed a little table beside the window overlooking the damp street. Mish rubbed her hands together, thankful for the heat, and breathing in the cosy coffee-tinged air. Winter was coming on fast that year, colder and wetter than the one before. She eyed her father's threadbare parka.

"So, how have you been?" she asked. Her father's face was lined with wear and his hair was greying, but his smile was wide and warm, exactly the same smile she remembered from her youth.

"I'm great, really great," he grinned easily at her. "But we can talk about me later. I want to hear what my girl has been up to."

"I'm good. Same old, you know?"

"Work's good?"

"It is," she told him about the Gutierrez siblings while he beamed at her. He was good at this bit: the enthusiasm for her work, his general amazement at her personality. Each time they met it was as if she had sprung into adulthood overnight to his delight and wonder. It was wonderful while it lasted and Mish couldn't help but enjoy it, albeit a little guiltily.

"That's brilliant, Pumpkin, really," he said, his face the picture of a proud father. "My successful girl. And your personal life? Any boys I should be meeting?"

Mish snorted at the notion that any companion of a woman her age would be called a 'boy'. Not to mention the idea that she would spring her father on any such unlucky soul. "Not so much,"

"Good," he said, crossing his arms sternly. Mish played along, letting him be the overly protective father looking out for his little girl.

"Now tell me about you," Mish said. "How's Linda?"

Her father's smile shifted. "Well, that I don't know. Lindy and I, ah, we're not involved anymore."

Mish's smile stiffened. "Well, that's a shame," she said.

"I guess," he scoffed.

"Where are you staying, then?" Mish pressed.

"Here and there," he said. "You know me. I get by."

Mish bit her lip, shifting her gaze to the street outside the window. A man outside was fighting with his bike lock.

"You don't need to worry about me, kiddo," Henry said. Mish felt his calloused hand rest on her own. "I've got some good leads on a place. And - listen to this - I've got an interview. Roger got me in at the dealership. It's as good as set. I've just got to show up for the interview and look presentable, that's it."

"That's wonderful, dad," said Mish, a flower of hope blooming in her chest. He did look better than usual. Maybe things were getting better.

"It will be, yeah," he said. "Just worried about the 'presentable' bit, but you know I clean up pretty nice. I mean, do I wish I had the fancy suit? Sure. But you make do with what you've got."

There it was. Why couldn't he ever just come out and ask for money? It was always this rigmarole of him hinting and talking around it until Mish gave in and offered. Even then he would make her work for it, holding out until she insisted. That way it was her idea, his daughter being generous rather than him being a deadbeat.

"I told Roger, I said, 'You get what you see with me' I'm a simple man, but I work hard, and I always come out on top," he continued. "Not much flash, but I get the job done. I think those are our coffees-,"

Mish watched him make his way to the coffee bar, swallowing down the lump in her throat, doing mental calculations. A job was imperative if Linda was gone. She imagined he had spent the last month couch hopping on friends' quickly waning charity. A job meant stability. Was it a sales position? He would need clothes for something like that. Customers wouldn't appreciate his moth-eaten sweaters.

"How much would a suit cost?" she asked when he returned with their steaming mugs in hand.

"A suit?" he set the mugs on the table. "I can't ask you to do that."

Mish smiled stiffly. *I haven't offered yet.* But she said "You'll need something nice once you start working anyway. How much?"

"Oh, Pumpkin, wow, I - thank you," he said, beaming. Mish felt a rush of accomplishment. Deep down she was still that little girl desperate for her father's approval. "My kind little girl. Two hundred should do it."

Mish blanched. Money like that was going to make her monthly budget tight. "I'll transfer it."

"Thank you, honey. Really," he said.

"No problem," said Mish, feigning confidence as she sipped her chai latte.

"No, I really appreciate it," he said "Really, you are too kind. I can swing by the shop on my way back tonight," He eyed her expectantly.

Mish took the hint. She pulled out her phone and made the transfer.

He rambled for the rest of their meeting about his plans for this or that. Mish wasn't really listening. She was busy recalculating her expenses and figuring out what she could cut to make her bills at the end of the month. Still, she didn't regret it. It would be worth it if he landed a job.

They parted soon after. Her father crushed her into a big bear hug, thanking her over and over again and promising to call her after the interview. Mish's gaze followed him as he disappeared down the street, whistling himself a jaunty little tune. She was relieved to see him happy, but she couldn't shake the nagging stress that she had done something wrong.

She thought about it at the grocery store where she picked up bags of rice and beans, deciding she could eat light to make ends meet. She thought about it when her boss called to congratulate her on securing Shelly's placement and scheduled a check in on the Gutierrezes in a month. And she thought about it while she was making her way back to the tube, her phone tucked on her shoulder by her ear and her shopping in hand - her boss ranting about form revisions.

"I'm sorry, Daphne," said Mish, noticing a figure across the street. "I have to go. I'll call you back"

She hung up and stomped across the road, ignoring the cars honking and screeching to a stop to avoid her. Her father sat on a stoop, head in his hands.

"Are you alright?" she asked, though she knew the answer.

He looked up and Mish gasped. His left eye was swollen shut, a bruise already blossoming under the skin, and his lip was split. His remaining eye widened when he realised it was her.

"My God, what happened to you?" she dropped onto the stoop next to him, clasping his hand in hers.

"I'm fine, just resting a moment," he waved her off. Mish's eyes darted around the street looking for the culprit or maybe someone to help.

She wasn't sure. Her gaze caught on the shopfront behind them, and her heart pounded in her ears.

"Resting in front of a betting shop?"

"Now, I know what this probably looks like, Pumpkin-."

"Don't 'Pumpkin' me, dad," she snapped. "Tell me what you did."

The lines on his face deepened in the cloudy overhead light, made all the worse by his bruising. The stoop of his shoulders showed Mish a frailty she'd never seen in him, the way he held his hands close to his chest.

"I had a little bet on the races - a great tip, seemed like solid info," he said, his eyes trained on his feet.

"Jesus, dad," Mish felt sick and stupid standing there with her rice and beans, visions of her father's new job still dancing in her head.

"How was I supposed to know the information was shit?" he said.

"I'm pretty sure that's the point of betting," Mish said.

The mask came off, the vulnerability lasting only a moment as his face twisted into an angry glare.

"I don't know who you think you are talking to me like that," he snapped nastily. "I am your father-,"

"You *stole* from me, dad," said Mish, her throat tight. She swallowed hard against the lump in her throat, determined not to cry.

"Oh, I'm a thief now? I would never have taken it if I knew you were going to act like this."

A cold resignation washed over her then. He was never going to see his wrongdoing. He wasn't capable of seeing past a potential windfall. She knew that when she offered him that money. God, she could have kicked herself. How many times did they need to play out the old dance before she stopped letting him let her down? How long until it stopped hurting when he did?

"How much did you lose?" she asked. Her voice sounded small and sad to her ears.

"Don't pretend you give a shit," he snapped.

Mish didn't react, just stared at the traffic on the street. She couldn't look at him and say what she needed to say. "Whoever beat you is going to do it again if you don't come up with the money. Was it just the two hundred?"

To her absolute horror, he placed his head in his hands and sobbed. Great heaving sobs like a child. It took everything in Mish not to recoil from him. She felt a shameful twist of disgust. Followed by guilt at feeling the disgust in the first place. For all his faults, he was still her father.

"How much?" she said again.

"I borrowed from the house when I lost the money," he said, wiping his nose disgustingly on his sleeve. "I was going to win it back-,"

"*How much,*"

"Twenty-four hundred," he snapped, his voice suddenly clear.

"Jesus Christ," Mish said. Her head fell back, and she stared at the sky above her, wishing it would swallow her up. "Jesus fucking Christ."

He sobbed into his hands again. "I know. I know I'm a fuck up. I try so hard to get it together. I want to be better for you, Pumpkin, I really do."

Mish thought about how easily she could vomit on the street right then. He was infuriatingly pathetic, and she was even worse for capitulating to it. *Mum doesn't get involved in this anymore*, she thought. *Uncle Thomas doesn't talk to him. They know better, and I should know by now too.* Her stomach was roiling, her heart pounding a hole in her chest, and she wanted nothing more than to crawl under a blanket and disappear. But she couldn't. Because he was her father and was sick and his lip was split and the people that did this to him were going to do much worse when he couldn't pay up.

Mish was crying, silent tears slipping down her cheeks. He didn't notice though. He was too wrapped up in his performance as Gambling Addict #1. She wiped her eyes inconspicuously.

"I'll take care of it," she said. It would completely drain her savings and she had no idea how she would be able to make rent that month. Worst case scenario she could call Uncle Thomas and ask for a loan. Although, the idea of explaining what she needed the money for brought on a fresh wave of nausea. Or maybe she'd take him up on his job offer after all. Either way she couldn't leave her father for dead on the street.

"You will?" he was nauseatingly relieved. "Oh, Pumpkin-."

She stopped him from speaking, grabbing both of his hands and gripping them hard.

"I *need* you to be okay. Do you understand?" she held his gaze, pleading with him. "Please. I need this to end."

"Of course, Pumpkin," he said, his face breaking into a smile. "I just hit a low point. I always bounce back."

Mish pulled away, standing and gathering her things so she could go inside and pay her father's loan sharks. Nothing was going to change. He was following a script, saying all the right things to manipulate her. And what was worse was that she knew he was doing it and she let him anyway. She would always let him. Except maybe there would be a time that she didn't get there in time, when she wouldn't find him crying on the street, when he got more than a split lip. The thought chilled her.

She eyed her father. It was as if the sobbing man on the stoop had never existed. He bounded to his feet and opened the door for her. But he wasn't the hopeful man from the coffee shop either. The charade was over. The grift was run. He'd got what he came for and gutted Mish in the process. He had seen the light at the end of the tunnel.

TEN

Grey was roused the next day by the gentle sound of wind chimes. He groaned, wrapping his arms tighter around Mish and burying his head in her hair.

"That's the alarm," she said, her voice thickly sleepy. Grey melted, suddenly so grateful to have woken beside her. Mish, sex-rumpled and barely woken, was magnificent.

"How did you get chimes?" he asked with a yawn. "My room yells 'Good Morning' every day,"

Mish giggled and wiggled away from him. "You just change the setting. Let me up-," He groaned again, opening his eyes just in time to see her wrap herself in a blanket to walk across the room and spin the alarm disk.

"There are settings?" he asked. "Nobody told me there are settings,"

"Of course there are settings. Jesus, Grey, you're really showing your age here," she winked at him.

"I would like to take this opportunity to remind you that you are the oldest person present," he said.

She stuck her tongue out at him. "Respect your elders, young man,"

They washed together and ate some of the abandoned fruit from the night before. Overall Grey felt much better than expected. His head was a little sore, but his body felt delightfully loose and relaxed. His whole demeanour, really. It was like waking up in a dream. After months of longing for her, now he could reach out and touch Mish without thinking. He took full advantage, kissing her cheek when she reached across the table for another apple slice, wrapping his arms around her waist while she tried to pull on her grey uniform. He couldn't keep his hands off of her.

She seemed to feel the same. She tangled her fingers with his as she ate, ran her fingers through his hair and scratched his scalp when he hugged her. They might have been waking up together for months with how easily they moved around each other now.

"What should we tell the others?" she asked when at last it came time to leave for work.

Grey studied her, nervous that he might see a flash of hesitancy or regret. But her eyes met his steadily.

"Well, this isn't exactly *casual* for me," he said, swallowing nervously. This was all new to him, this intimacy and comfort. His previous relationships had been all about constant evaluation, always looking ahead to make sure his partners fit the next step in his life. Things were different now. He didn't care if Mish fit his idea of his life, he was willing to do anything to fit hers. "I mean, I'll go along with whatever you're comfortable with, but as far as I'm concerned, I'm yours. If you'll have me,"

She kissed him then and it was soft and sweet and so perfect that he wished he could live in the moment forever.

"It's not casual for me, either then," she said against his lips.

They disentangled from each other after a while. The wind chimes gently warned them that they were approaching tardiness, so they made their way to the break room hand in hand.

"Hey, Grey?" Mish said as they crossed the breezeway. It was raining and he could barely hear her over the roar of the waterfall.

"Yes, Mish?" he said.

"That crypto you were talking about last night. What was it called?"

Grey raised an eyebrow. "Arcanum. Why?"

"Just wondering," said Mish lightly. "I thought - I thought maybe I'd heard of it before."

"Have you?" he asked, raising their joined hands to kiss her knuckles.

She smiled a little sadly. "No. No, I don't think so."

Mish was quiet for the rest of the morning. Grey would have blamed it on the nerves of coming out as a couple, but the guys took the situation in stride. Mark let out a low whistle when they walked in and offered up an amused "About time," while Ishaan grinned in the corner and Matthias asked what he had missed. Troy nodded, for his part, though he looked a little too green to be taking in much of anything going on around him.

The rain prevented them from cleaning the solar panels as planned, so their supervising guard led them to the research and development labs to clean the machinery. It was a more mindless task than most and Grey found his mind wandering to Mish. There was definitely something on her mind. He knew her well enough by now to know that she was never this quiet. He tried to catch her eye several times, but she was fixated on the task at hand.

"Women," Mark mouthed over her shoulder. Grey rolled his eyes good-naturedly. Whatever was bothering her, he was pretty sure it wasn't him.

They broke for lunch and made their way to the canteen, and Grey was careful to let the others pass them in the hallway.

"You alright?" Grey asked once they were alone.

Mish blinked up at him a little dazedly. "What do you mean?"

"You're being very quiet," said Grey. "Maybe a little distracted. Is it me? Is this too fast, or-?"

"No, my goodness, of course not," she laughed. "I've just been thinking…," she trailed off again, her eyes searching his face. She bit her lip.

"Thinking about?"

"Do you remember the password thing? For Arcanum?" she asked.

It was Grey's turn to blink. "The seed phrase? Er, I think so?"

"Are you sure? Could you say it now?"

Grey's knee-jerk reaction was to get defensive. He swallowed his shame, realising that the Grey of the past would have and actually did take that money to his grave. It wasn't in his old nature to share assets. But Mish was looking up at him with those eyes so full of trust, her thumb tracing those little circles in his palm again…

Grey strained to remember. He hoped the reanimation process hadn't destroyed any of the neural connections in his memory. He found himself thinking of mushy defrosted meat.

"Route. Wing. Oven…Addition. Hole. Carpenter. Sink. Cattle. Position…Candle. Chance. Page," he said.

Mish's eyes widened almost imperceptibly. "Are you sure?"

"Pretty sure, yeah," Grey said, rubbing the back of his neck. "What does it matter?"

"I think I have an idea," she said.

Grey's heart skipped a beat. "What kind of idea?"

Mish licked her lips and glanced around the corridor nervously.

"I don't want to talk about it here," she said. "There are too many people who could be listening, and I don't want to get your hopes up."

"What are you-,"

"I'll come to your room tonight," she said. "After dinner. I should have it sorted by then," Mish kissed him on the cheek and walked off in the opposite direction. "I'll see you tonight!" she called back and disappeared around the corner and out of sight.

*

Mish didn't return for the after-lunch shift with the rest of them.

Grey worried about her, wondering where she had gone and whether any guards were giving her trouble. None of the Maintenance team had ever been sick before - a testament to the food and overall health afforded them by reanimation he was sure - and he didn't know what precedence there was for walking off in the middle of a shift. Now that he was thinking about it, he wasn't sure what disciplinary proceedings were in place. Was there a jail full of Rainies somewhere? Or did they, heaven forbid, send their delinquents to that horrible battlefield as penance?

"I can feel you freaking out over there," Mark said, interrupting Grey's thoughts.

"I'm not freaking out," said Grey. He scrubbed at the floor vigorously, taking out his anxiety on the scuff marks in the polished concrete.

"I'm sure she's fine," Mark said. "Saint Mish wouldn't just disappear on you,"

"Yeah," said Grey. "Yeah, you're probably right,"

He kept his head down for the rest of the day, just barely listening to the conversation around him, his mind fixated on Mish. What could she be planning? The Arcanum account was long gone by now, he was sure of it. The counsellor all but told him as much. Besides, since when was Mish interested in money?

Finally, the shift ended, and Grey followed the others to the canteen for dinner. He picked at his food half-heartedly. He couldn't make himself eat; his appetite was gone. He wasn't alone in his discomfort, at least. Troy's colour had returned sometime after lunch, but he too picked at his food, sipping a seltzer, and sticking to starches.

Back in his room Grey paced anxiously. The time was trickling by slowly, but Grey was certain something was keeping Mish away. She should have been there by now. It was after dinner and Mish was never late. He threw himself on his bed and stared at the ceiling trying to quell his frustration. This was exactly why he hated surprises; the lack of control made him crazy.

"Visitor," said his room.

"Thank God," he said, twisting the door disk before his room had time to speak again. There was Mish, eyes bright and cheeks flushed, her hair a mess of windswept curls. He drew her to him, wrapping his arms around her and inhaling her scent, so impossibly relieved to have her in his arms. That she was safe. "Where have you been?" he sighed into her hair.

"I brought you something," she said breathlessly. She broke away from him as the door slid shut and pulled a small, book-shaped package from her pocket.

"What is it?"

"Open it," she was practically buzzing with energy.

He pulled the ribbon free with shaking hands and opened the box. Inside was a tablet, a syringe, and four tiny vials filled with a yellowish liquid.

"I don't understand," he said.

"Turn it on," she insisted. "Just run your thumb along the bottom there."

Grey did as he was told and the tablet hummed to life, projecting a welcome screen into the air. The MerryCom symbol spun in mid-air for a moment before dissolving into a different message.

'Travel Plans - 1 Day Pass' said the screen.

"Day pass?" Grey said, his mouth uncomfortably dry. "How did you-? You got me a day pass to the outside world? Why would you get me a day pass?"

"Don't freak out," Mish said, drawing him to sit on the bed next to her. "I asked around, and not only does Arcanum still exist, but its offices aren't far from here. I knew it sounded familiar, Arcanum was getting big in my time, and now they basically manage the currency that the Protos use today."

Grey couldn't speak. He could only look between the projection and Mish in absolute disbelief.

"I realised that all we need to do is get you there and they can help you find the wallet, if you explain it to them," she said in a heady rush. "So, I used my credits and I got you a pass. It came with the tablet, which will lead you to the facility, and inoculations. Apparently, they only update ours so far while we're still in debt."

Grey's stomach dropped. "Mish," he said, his voice ragged. "How much did this cost you?"

Two spots of pink appeared on Mish's cheeks. "It doesn't matter."

"It does." he said.

"Just about all three years," she said, looking anywhere but at him. "But it doesn't matter, don't you see? If you get that wallet, we can both get out of here. Consider it a loan with an extraordinarily high rate of interest."

"Don't joke about this," Grey groaned. He ran his hands through his hair, pulling at his scalp. "I can't accept this."

"You have to,"

"I *won't* accept this," he revised. "It's too much, Mish. It's too risky. What if I have the seed phrase wrong? What if the wallet isn't there anymore? You can't ask me to risk your credits - three years of your life - on a chance like that."

"You're not risking anything, I am!"

"That's exactly what I'm talking about," said Grey. "You didn't even talk to me. You didn't plan properly. You're giving up everything on a gamble!"

Mish reacted as if he had slapped her, flinching away from the word. "Don't lecture me, Grey."

"I'm not-,"

"You are," she said. "Besides, what's done is done."

"I really appreciate it, Mish. Really, I do. This is so generous of you and I love you for it," said Grey. "But you need to take it back. Get a refund."

"There are no refunds," she said, stubbornly.

Silence hung in the air. Palpable.

"Please, Grey," she said softly. "I need this. I'm suffocating down here. I need to see the world again. I need to know that there's something to look forward to after this. Every day I walk across that breezeway I get closer and closer to jumping."

Grey paled at that. His heart was pounding in his throat at the thought. And how had he missed it?

"I had no idea," said Grey. He was aching to hold her, but he wasn't sure she would appreciate the gesture. Her arms were crossed tightly against her chest and her whole body was shivering. She was as close to crying as Grey had ever seen her. "I didn't know,"

"I didn't want you to know," she said. "I didn't want anybody to know because that would make it real. Grey, this money, it's a lifeline. I could barely sleep last night thinking of the possibilities,"

"Okay," said Grey.

"Okay?" Mish's bottom lip trembled.

"I'll go. If it's what you need, of course I'll go," he ran a hand across his face. "But what if the money isn't there?"

Mish gave him a watery smile, tears finally spilling over her cheeks. "Then we'll serve out our sentences together. We'll finish around the same time now."

He kissed her, crushing her against him, trying desperately to communicate how grateful he was, how he needed her as much as she needed him to take a chance on the money being there. They broke apart, panting, but he held her close, his forehead pressed to hers and his heart pounding as the reality sunk in.

If he could pull this off, they would both be leaving MerryCom.

ELEVEN

"Do you have everything?" asked Mish. She was practically vibrating as she walked beside him, the excitement bubbling up from somewhere deep inside her. It was a side of Mish that he had never seen before, Mish with a refreshed purpose. This Mish was glowing with decisive dedication, every feature sharpened with hope. Grey imagined that this was the Mish her clients experienced as a social worker and was left with a weary, unbalanced feeling that in that moment she was a stranger to him. That this was only the beginning of the unknowable depths inside of her.

"I think so," he said, shifting the pack on his shoulder. It was sore from the inoculations the night before. 23rd century vaccines were no joke. The backpack was a horrible beige thing graciously loaned by the company to carry his packed lunch for the day and stamped with the MerryCom logo. It clashed horribly with his grey uniform, something that would have driven the old Grey absolutely mad. This Grey, however, was more preoccupied with the lump in his stomach as they made their way across the breezeway.

"Don't be nervous," pressure on his hand as Mish squeezed. "You're going to do great."

Grey nodded, schooling his features into what he hoped was a convincing smile. She was comforting herself as much as she was trying to comfort him. Those were her credits on the line and, as much as she presented bravado, the reality of what she stood to lose was starkly obvious in the daylight.

They fell into delicate silence and followed their guard escort down the familiar tangle of hallways with hands intertwined. Grey's mind was spinning. He couldn't voice a coherent thought if he tried. He pictured Mish in the canteen hallway, the way she kissed him and sprinted off to make the most irrational decision he could imagine. The wild gamble for her freedom. It nauseated him that she would risk her future on a whim and, if he was honest, that she was capable of acting so recklessly.

But, underneath all of that discomfort, Grey clung to Mish's hand like a lifeline as they made their way to MerryCom's transportation bay. He was complete in the understanding that he would do anything to secure her future. To see her safely ensconced with her cooking and her work and, with any luck, him.

The transportation bay doors slid open revealing something resembling a train platform from Grey's time. The vehicle inside, however, bore little resemblance to the trains of his past. Instead of rails and metal, there was a smooth white pod suspended in mid-air.

"Magnets?" he murmured. Mish winked at him as the guard pushed past them and typed something into their tablet.

"Delta-A Mark 137?" said the guard. Grey and Mish waited in polite silence until it became clear that the guard was talking to them.

"Oh, am I Delta whatever?" asked Grey. "You can call me Grey,"

"Delta-A Mark 137. Day pass issue 5923394, can you confirm?" said the guard.

"Er, yeah. Confirm, I guess," said Grey, retrieving his tablet from the backpack and presenting the hologram. He assumed the guard made a note of it, but it was difficult to see what they were looking at when they wore those terrible helmets.

"This transport will take you to the main bay at the base of the mountain. From there you will board ride-share 42C into town. Do you understand?" said the guard.

"Yes," Grey's voice came out in a dry croak and he tightened his grip on Mish's hand. Faced with the real world, Grey was seized with sudden desperation to keep her with him.

"Your day pass expires in 12 hours. You are to report to this transport bay no later than 7:24 pm. Do you understand?"

"Yes," Grey repeated.

"What if he's late?" Mish asked.

"He won't be," said the guard.

"If there's a transportation delay or-,"

"There are no delays," said the guard with an air of finality that pressed them into silence.

Mish met Grey's eyes worriedly, her lip caught between her teeth as she looked up at him. He traced her cheek with his thumb, his wariness momentarily replaced with the urge to comfort her, and he realised that it wasn't the enormity of the gesture or the gamble that worried him. The unpredictability of the action triggered that old part of him that needed to control everything and everybody. The relief of letting that go was overwhelming. He pulled her closer and kissed her gently, reverently.

"You may board," said the guard. The pod seemed to undulate, the smooth wall rearranging itself until a round doorway appeared on the side revealing a singular seat that Grey assumed was meant for him.

"Be safe, said Mish softly in his ear. "I'll be here when you get back,"

Once he was safely strapped into the pod, the wall reformed itself. From the inside the pod was translucent, so Grey could see the entire transport bay as if he were looking through cheesecloth. Mish was clenching and unclenching her fists, pitched slightly forward on her toes as if her nervous energy was going to send her sprinting at any moment. The guard remained as impassive as ever.

Grey only had time for one last look at Mish before there was a soft beeping sound and the transport shot out of the bay. It moved so smoothly that Grey could only comprehend the speed by watching the lights outside flash by. He swallowed queasily and was just beginning to wonder if he was experiencing motion sickness when the transport slowed to a stop in a much bigger, more crowded bay.

Grey unbuckled his straps and stumbled out of the transport on rubbery legs as soon as the door opened, relieved to feel solid ground again. The relief was short-lived. As soon as his stomach settled and Grey was able to take in his surroundings it became overwhelmingly apparent how *different* the world had become.

This bay was a massive snarl of walkways, food stalls, and transport vehicles that positively dwarfed the one he had just exited. Above him the ceiling was a strange glass that dilated and darkened in waves, momentarily obscuring the blue sky with its picture-perfect puffy white clouds. And there were people. More people than Grey had come in contact with in the entirety of his time in the Ark and at the MerryCom campus. People walking in groups or talking into their tablets, wearing clothing made from pearly materials Grey didn't recognise, eating food Grey had never seen before. Laughing, crying, talking, shouting, singing. The wave of noise was an unsettling roar in Grey's ears, and he inhaled a gulp of fresh air, willing himself to focus on the sweet, clean scent and not to remember the mud and stink of the battlefield.

Grey made his way through the crowd toward the transport conveniently labelled Rideshare 42C, grateful that his simple task appeared to actually be simple for once. He felt a prickle at the back of his neck. Were people purposefully avoiding his path or was he imagining it? The crowd seemed to bubble around him, so his way was mostly unimpeded. He caught more than a couple of suspicious glances, but he squared his shoulders and continued on. His awful, colourless uniform stuck out against the mass of colour and textures worn by the people around him and he felt a stirring of insecurity that he had never experienced before. The Grey of the past would have fit in here, standing in silent judgement of the poor, stupid, unskilled worker in the ugly uniform with no idea where he was supposed to go.

He approached the rideshare, adjusting his pack on his shoulder. The shifting weight was enough to distract him from the stares of the people around him. He reached what he assumed to be the front at the same time as another man, this one short and stocky and wearing some sort of suit with a cape. Grey eyed the cape, unable to decide if it served function or fashion. The man stared right back, his face stiff and emotionless. After a moment, he gestured for Grey to proceed ahead of him. The gesture was almost kind, but Grey suspected it was really a test. A test he was about to fail. Faced with the storey-high white wall of the rideshare, Grey had no idea how to board the damn thing. He scanned the wall for a familiar iridescent disk but found none.

"Useless," the man said, pushing past Grey to insert his tablet into an opening that Grey had missed. The door slipped open, and the man stomped onto the transport with an impatient shake of his head.

Humiliation prickled across Grey's scalp, but he followed suit, inserting his tablet and retrieving it as the door slid open to accommodate him. The inside of the transport was dotted with passengers tucked into seats placed sporadically about the cabin. Grey glanced around, desperate to be seated where he couldn't draw more attention to himself, but all of the seats were taken. He made his way to the back of the transport, avoiding the caped man's eyes as he passed.

A woman toward the back of the transport did *something* with her hands and a seat popped into existence. Grey leaned against the wall and looked surreptitiously at his fellow passengers. Watching them spring their own seats into existence while he fumed at his own incompetence. It was like his first month at the Ark all over again. He was seized by a horrible fear that he would never catch up. That the world would always be a thousand steps ahead and he would be notable only in his obsolescence. The object of ridicule, with a red face glowing in tow. Unable to open a door or find a seat.

"It's a hand scanner," said a voice to his right. A young woman was speaking from her seat behind him. Her eyes widened nervously when they met Grey's, but she gestured for him to hold his palm out in front of him as if he was pressing on an invisible door. He did as he was told and sure enough a seat appeared next to him.

"Thank you," he said, but the woman had pointedly turned away from him. In fact, the majority of his traveling companions seemed unwilling to look his way. Stigmatised and ratted out by his MerryCom uniform, Grey settled in his seat, backpack situated in his lap, missing Mish, and overwhelmed by the world around him.

The rideshare was made with the same translucent material as the earlier transport and Grey marvelled at his surroundings as they left the transport bay. Here was the green utopia he had been promised. The landscape was changed from his time - the climate was warmer, closer to a tropical environment than the cool, misty London of his past. *If this ever was London,* he thought with a pang, realising that he didn't even know which continent he was on.

They passed under a massive tangle of trees taller and wider than the skyscrapers he remembered from his past. Grey stared up at the leafy canopy, amazed to see houses and buildings tucked among the branches. Below his feet a river snaked through the forest with water so clear that Grey could make out the smear of pebbles on the bottom. There were no roads, no cars belching their gasses into the atmosphere, only the occasional transport zoomed past them utilising whatever clean energy magic this society had managed to harness. It wasn't possible, but there it was. Perfect. Nature and humanity were in harmony at last. And yet…

Where was the battlefield? Where were the slums?

Grey knew what he had seen. Did these people know that the clean life they lived was paid for with the life of an old man shot like a dog and left to die in the mud? He clenched his hands together in his lap, focusing on his calloused palms to block out the sudden rush of rage detonating in his chest.

The rideshare pulled into a new bay, this one in the centre of a sprawling cityscape carved from sandstone. The buildings were dotted with gardens and sprinkled with tree life and a massive fountain trilled with clean water. He lifted his palm to vanish his seat and made his way to the door of the transport.

"Move," somebody shouldered him to the side, and he went sprawling to the ground, instinctively clutching onto strangers' clothes as he fell. People turned and Grey scrambled to his feet furiously, but his assailant had already disappeared into the crowd. He was attracting attention again, people around him shuffling away nervously, some even glaring in his direction.

"*Rainy*," somebody hissed.

Grey ducked his head and stormed through the crowd, his shoulders squared and stiff. He stormed through the gate that demarcated the beginning of the open-air transport bay. Outside the air was maddeningly sweet with the perfume of the flower beds. The sun overhead was bright as he made his way down the sandstone wall and through a quiet alley, squinting his eyes in the glare. Grey pinched the bridge of his nose, trying in vain to stave off the beginnings of a headache. On the ground, the alley was lined with optimistic little white flowers. He leaned against the wall, the sandstone warm on his back. The smells were strange, the people were hostile to him, and Grey would have given anything to see something - *anything* - he recognised. Even a drunk passed out in a puddle of his own sick would have been a comfort from this pristine beige and green utopia. Or, as it seemed to be for a Rainy, more of a dystopia.

Transitional periods can be difficult, his counsellor had said. She might have been on to something with those useless glasses and pen. But she hadn't known, couldn't really know, how overwhelming it was. Grey felt infantile in his discomfort and the thought enraged him.

His hand shook as he unzipped his pack and booted up his navigation card. If the blinking cursor was any indication, the Arcanum building was close. Grey stared at the map with the stirrings of excitement. What if his money - his social, as well as actual, currency - really was there? He took a deep breath, wary of his own excitement. What would it be like to be turned away again? How would he face Mish if her gamble didn't pay off?

Back on the street, navigation card in hand, Grey snaked along what he determined to be the road based on its relative orientations to the buildings around it. There didn't appear to be any street signs, at least nothing Grey would have recognised as such, which made following the map difficult. The blinking cursor updated his position and highlighted his route ahead of him but didn't account for overgrown brush or portions of the street blocked off for large groups to picnic or dance or whatever seemed to catch their fancy at a given moment. And his tablet seemed to be an older model that had difficulty connecting with the card at all, so occasionally the map would disappear altogether.

"Excuse me, can you point me to the Arcanum building?" he finally stopped and asked a gentleman covered head to toe in finger paint, carefully applied in dots and swirls across his skin by his equally colourful companion.

The man's eyes narrowed with contempt. "What's the matter, Rainy? Can't read?" and he gestured angrily for Grey to move along. Grey's jaw was sore with how violently he ground his teeth together, but he shook his head and pressed on. For Mish.

The next time he kept it simple, shaking his navigation card at a couple walking opposite him. "Arcanum?" he asked.

"Up the road another block," said the man kindly enough, though his arm tightened around his companion's waist. Like Grey was a threat. Like he was seconds away from lunging across the street and attacking them.

"Thank you," Grey said, deciding to stick to his manners even if they were proving to be out of fashion. He turned away from the couple and walked right into a wall of a man who had been standing way too close. The man in turn bumped into the woman beside him, who scoffed at Grey.

"What are you-?" the man sputtered, rounding on Grey. His face twisted into a glare as he took in Grey's uniform. To Grey's absolute horror, the man looked him up and down, sneered out *"Earth killing savage,"* and then spat on Grey's shirt.

Grey stared at the spittle soaking into the fabric of his uniform as the man stomped away, shaking all over. So that was it. The hostility, the glares - all of it a reaction to who he was. What he was. An earth-killing Rainy. Whatever his people had done to the planet must have been harder to come back from than any of them in the Ark had imagined. This outrage must have laid the building blocks for the carbon tax that kept them all enslaved to the Ark. Though Grey wasn't sure the Ark had felt like a prison to him for a long time.

The Arcanum building was a masterpiece of glass and stone architecture, spiralling to the treetops in a great sheet that reflected the street below in the afternoon sun. Grey might have dismissed it as some government building if it hadn't been for the fountain in front whose cascading water formed the Arcanum symbol from his past. *Thank goodness they never changed that logo,* he thought.

Grey climbed the ivy-covered stairs, his stomach tangled with anxiety. Or excitement. It was hard to tell the difference anymore. When he reached the door, it slid open silently, hastening him inside where the floor was polished to a streak-free shine that screamed luxury. The building reminded him of Piety Financial. Not in aesthetics, but rather in the way it seemed to gleam with its own opulence. No matter the architectural and technological changes, wealth was wealth, and Arcanum was glazed with it.

"Name?" asked a silvery screen situated behind a marble desk in what could only be described as an entrance hall. Two glass staircases framed the desk and climbed out of sight, their bannisters shining with braided silver made to look like the roots of a tree.

"Er, Graham Wright," Grey coughed, leaning forward awkwardly just in case the screen couldn't see him properly. "Grey,"

"Welcome, Er Graham Wright Grey," said the screen and a little name tag popped out of a theretofore invisible opening. Grey grabbed it reluctantly, eyeing the misspelling with frustration.

"Just Grey, actually," he said through gritted teeth.

Another name tag popped out, this one reading *Justgrey Actually*. Grey rolled his eyes and pinned the first tag onto his shirt, careful to avoid the dried spittle. His chest still felt a little clammy where the stranger's saliva had soaked through.

"Purpose?" asked the screen.

"Speak to a person," said Grey as if he was talking to an automated phone line back in his time.

"Purpose?" said the screen again.

"*Person*," said Grey.

There was a beat of silence while the screen considered him.

"Staircase to the right, please," it said finally.

A luminous arrow appeared from deep within a recess of the polished floor directing him in the right direction.

"Thank you," said Grey. He was rewarded with another name tag, predictably reading *Thank You*. Grey ignored it and made his way to the staircase which seemed to stretch into infinity. Would the arrow on the floor direct him the rest of the way? He glanced back at the screen but, finding no clarification there, made his way to the stairs.

No sooner had his foot planted on the second step than the entire staircase began moving. It was almost like the escalators Grey remembered, except instead of all of the stairs acting as a conveyor belt of sorts, these stairs seemed to pixelate and slide him along his way. It moved quickly, zooming him up floors and past hallways faster than he could count. Then, as quickly as it had started, it stopped, depositing him on a landing that led to a short hallway. He exited the moving staircase, which re-pixeled itself into normality, and followed the hallway to a door that he pried open gingerly.

Behind the door was another desk and behind the desk was, thankfully, a person. She was middle-aged with her hair fashioned into a massive beehive that might have looked perfect in the 60s were it not for its unusual turquoise colour. The combination of the lined face with the youthful hair was fascinating. There had been vibrant hair on people in the street and terminal as well, but none of them seemed to maintain theirs with the same whimsical dedication. Her eyes were downcast, trained on her tablet. Grey cleared his throat, not wanting to startle her.

"I know you're here. I can hear a door opening," she said sharply, her watery eyes darting up to him.

"Right, sorry," said Grey bashfully.

"How can I help you?" she asked, sweet yet sharp again.

"I'm sorry to bother you," said Grey, nervous with her unblinking eyes trained on him. "I just, it's difficult to explain. That's why I asked for a person so, thank you. For helping me, I mean."

She raised one eyebrow. How long had it been since she'd blinked? It was becoming unsettling.

"I, um, I bought crypto from this company. Arcanum, I mean. A long time ago," said Grey. "Two hundred years ago, actually."

"I'm unfamiliar," was all she said.

"I was worried about that," said Grey, the coil in his stomach tightening. "It's, it *was* a type of asset… money really. Cryptocurrency? It would be saved in a wallet. A really old account with a seed phrase key."

"Follow me," she said.

"Thank y-," Grey gasped, his voice catching in his throat as she made her way around the desk. What he had mistaken for a woman was really a woman's torso affixed to a tall grey box that zoomed just above the floor, similarly to the canvas trash bags back at MerryCom.

"Is there a problem?" she asked pointedly.

"Are you a-?" Grey cut himself off, aware that he was being terribly rude but unable to stop himself.

"I am a robot assistant and database master key designed for this Arcanum base, yes," she said. This time Grey noticed the abnormal lilt to her voice. "Follow me," she said again, leading him back onto the stairs.

They zoomed past an unknown number of floors before coasting to a stop at another landing. This one led to an open waiting room where people sat in clusters and another robot woman, identical to the robot beside him, sat behind another desk.

"I've got a Re-Animated asking about financials from the 21st century," said his robot.

"Escalate to management," said the second, waiving them through a door to her right.

Behind that door was a hallway, bustling with Protos ducking in and out of the offices lining the walls. The robot directed Grey to sit on a bench off to the side while she spoke to a screen mounted on the wall.

"Re-Animated seeking financial statements from the 21st century. Cryptocurrency," she said. She seemed to take great meaning from the beeps and buzzes the screen replied with, nodding her head sagely.

"Stay here," she said before zooming away.

Grey did as he was told, clutching his backpack to his chest, exhausted. He could smell Mish's perfume on the bag from when she had packed it that morning and he missed her with an ache stronger than the pit of anxiety in his stomach.

"Excuse me," said a polite voice.

Grey looked up at a man who appeared to be in his early twenties and was carrying a stack of books. Grey blinked in surprise. He hadn't seen a physical book since reanimating.

"Hello," he said, his voice quiet, unsure if he could handle more Proto hostility.

"I'm Xander," said the man. "I'm a historian here at Arcanum. Did I hear you mention something about crypto?"

Grey's heart jumped to his throat. "You know what crypto is?"

Xander's eyes gleamed. "I do."

"Oh, thank goodness," Grey sighed. "Can you help me explain?"

"I doubt I could help you explain to these," he nodded in the direction the robot had left in. "Nobody here knows anything about the old web. It hasn't been used for anything serious since before the Collapse," said Xander. Grey's stomach sank. "But I might be able to help."

TWELVE

"Cryptocurrency still exists. Of course, we just call it currency," was the first thing Xander said when they reached his office. He ushered Grey into a space lined with bookshelves with papers and books piled on nearly every surface in a way that was nostalgically 21st century. Although the paper looked wrong to Grey, a little - plasticky, ghostlike? Xander pulled the door closed behind him and gestured to a little beverage cart underneath a window looking out over the treetops. "Tea?"

"Sure," said Grey, desperate for something to keep his hands occupied. They were shaking with his nervous energy.

"After the Environmental Collapse in the late 2090s, society radically shifted to make way for the Second Renaissance," continued Xander as he fussed with a pebble-shaped kettle. "Sorry, you probably know this. Will you stop me if you do? I don't know what MerryCom explain in their, uh, introductory materials."

Graham stayed quiet, too nervous to reply, so Xander continued. "Our beliefs on ownership and wealth had to change to rebuild. We ended up with a sort of modified capitalist framework with strong socialistic ideals and an expanded idea of which aspects of survival are owed to us by the society we exist in, but with an aspect of free-market in our social class systems."

"I'm sorry, not sure I understand what that means," admitted Grey, his cheeks warming.

Xander shrugged Grey's confusion away. "Socialised the way you were, in a time when people believed in individual ownership over altruism, I'm not sure you're capable of understanding this world, no offence intended. What's important here, is that there are echoes of the structures you are familiar with from your time present here and now. Currency is only worth what we perceive it to be worth, after all. You could be the richest man in the world, and it wouldn't mean a thing unless your peers agreed it did."

Grey accepted the tea Xander offered him gratefully. What did Xander just say he could be? The conversation was doing nothing to help his headache. "So, you're telling me that money is still very important, even in this sharing-is-caring world?"

Xander's mouth quirked up into a smile. "That's exactly what I'm telling you, yes."

"Great," said Grey earnestly. His hands were shaking with a different sort of energy now, rattling his teacup against the saucer.

"Now," said Xander, perching himself on the arm of his book-laden couch and sipping his own tea. "Why don't you explain what a Rainy like yourself wants to know about an archaic currency such as the old Arcanum token?"

Grey swallowed a gulp of tea and began to tell his story, for what he hoped would be one of the final times. It felt different than when he had drunkenly told Mish about his plans. Without the benefit of alcohol and the safety of intimacy, Grey couldn't help but feel self-conscious. Still, he plodded along for Mish's sake.

"Fascinating," said Xander when Grey finished. "Absolutely fascinating. Remarkably creative problem-solving. Truly, I'm impressed."

"Thank you," said Grey. The tips of his ears felt hot. "Though, I suppose Jeffrey deserves most of the credit," Grey looked out the window, overcome for a moment with curiosity about the man who had certainly been dead for at least the last hundred and fifty years. His kids, his wife - all victims of the very time Grey had been able to escape with his help.

Xander nodded sagely. "You must be a brilliant mind, all the same."

Grey grunted in response.

"Cryptocurrencies took over rather quickly," said Xander, changing the subject. "They really hit the mainstream in the early 2030's and became the primary mechanism for banking not too long after that. And you, you lucky bastard, bought into Arcanum, which took its time but owing partly to its greener attributes, became the technology that underpins the primary currency of the world today. Now, once the laymen got in on the game, a lot of the old securities changed. It's my understanding that seed phrases fell out of fashion just before the switch to the New Web in 2113. Something about people losing them or forgetting them."

"New web?" asked Grey.

"The old web was cannibalised by big corporations interested in pay-to-play access. With so many everyday activities hinging on access to the old web, there was a movement to make broadband access an inalienable right. And with it a new, more equitable data-storing structure. Enter; the New Web," said Xander.

"I see," said Grey. "Would Arcanum have a record of my account, then? If it's the primary currency of this time?"

"On the Old Web, yes," said Xander. "Or rather, no. Your Jeffrey was right. With the way the account was set up the money doesn't exist as far as they're concerned until it's activated with the seed phrase, which would only be possible on the Old Web."

"Schrodinger's millions," said Grey dryly.

Xander looked confused for a moment but moved on quickly. "Obviously this would present a problem had you not met the only historian in eighteen districts with a working collection of 21st century computers, which do of course have access to the Old Web… though it's really kept alive by hobbyists and archivists these days."

Grey's mouth was dry. "You mean-?"

The younger man was grinning with excitement. "I can't guarantee it'll work, Grey. But we can certainly take a look."

*

The computer was more advanced than anything Grey had used before, though it had echoes of his old familiar desktop. It was a feat of engineering, with a thin, opaque screen mounted on spindly legs like gossamer silk that operated via touchscreen that mimicked the mobile phones of his time. Still, Grey stumbled through, thankful that at the very least the language and symbols were something he recognised.

Xander paced eagerly behind Grey as he worked, thrilled to see a native user interact with the machine. He seemed to be under the impression that Grey could offer some special insight into the culture of the

21st century by how he poked at the screen. It might have been endearing if Grey hadn't already felt sick with anticipation.

"There it is," Grey was breathless as the familiar Arcanum logo rotated across the screen. He had downloaded the platform needed to activate his wallet.

Xander clapped him hard on the back. "Well done, chap."

Grey navigated the login screen with ease until he reached the input for the seed phrase. He was trembling all over now, hope slicing through him until he was dizzy with it.

'Read when others are home, cousin,' said Charlie. Please can Cat play?

Route. Wing. Oven. Addition. Hole. Carpenter. Sink. Cattle. Position. Candle. Chance. Page.

Twelve words typed with shaking fingers on an unfamiliar keyboard. Grey hit enter.

Incorrect.

The word didn't register at first. Grey stared at the screen, willing the letters to rearrange themselves into something that made sense to him. How could his phrase be incorrect? His account was *right there*.

He typed the seed phrase again. Twice more. With capitals, all capitals, no capitals, his keystrokes became more and more desperate with each failed attempt.

"Maybe try a different phrase?" suggested Xander.

Grey clamped his teeth together until pain shot through his jaw, his mind wheeling through his mnemonics.

Route and Wing for a bird. Was it definitely 'oven' next? He was pretty sure. Addition was the opposite of hole. You wouldn't call a carpenter to fix your sink. The cattle were in the correct position-

And suddenly he remembered. The word he had so much trouble remembering in the first place, not candle. Channel.

Route. Wing. Oven. Addition. Hole. Carpenter. Sink. Cattle. Position. Channel. Chance. Page.

"You got it," breathed Xander, coming to stand behind Grey so he could read over his shoulder. "Holy shit, you've got it!"

The Arcanum logo spun into a welcome screen that asked him to pause for updates. A little loading bar popped up notifying him that his balance was updating. It was all too much, watching that little green bar inch closer and closer to completion. Grey practically leapt to his feet and began pacing the room.

"Tell me," Grey gasped. He was certain that he was having a heart attack. The organ seemed desperate to bore a hole through his chest. His mouth tasted like pennies and the adrenaline was making him ill.

"Updating, updating…" said Xander.

"I changed my mind," said Grey. "Don't tell me."

"Almost-," Xander froze. His mouth fell open with a comically audible *pop*.

"*Well?*" Grey's voice was bordering on hysterical.

"I think you should sit." Xander swallowed hard, his gaze rising. "Your life is about to change, friend,"

"Is it there?" Grey asked, his voice coming out in one breathless gasp.

"It's here," said Xander.

"How much?" Grey licked his lips, eagerly. He had never been much for praying, but in that moment, he appealed to any higher power he could think of that the sum was large enough to cover his and Mish's debts.

"Well, it's hard to say really, as I don't know the exchange rate, two ticks" Xander whipped up his tablet to do a conversion.

Xander had gone a funny sort of greenish colour. He reached for his tea and Grey noted that his hands were shaking almost as badly as

Grey's. He tossed back the remainder of his cup as if it were liquor rather than tea and wiped the back of his hand over his mouth.

"You are a very wealthy man, Mr. Wright," he said shakily. "One of the wealthiest in existence, it would seem. How long did you say your sentence is?"

Grey's mind had been taken over by static. "Eleven years."

Xander's laughter rang through his office. He threw his head back and let loose, his shoulders shaking with mirth. "That is a fraction - merely a fraction of a decimal point in your balance," he wiped his eyes, his fit finally settling. "You can have the world, chum."

Grey sank onto the couch, his legs unwilling to support him as a wave of vertigo washed over him. He covered his eyes with his hands, blocking the room from view. He needed to catch his breath. It felt as if he was falling from a great height, with stomach thumping, euphoric panic. He could see it: the house, Mish in the kitchen, Mish in his bed, Mish every morning and every night when they could belong entirely and only to each other. And, if he looked closely enough, there was a child.

He might have been laughing or crying. It was impossible to tell. Great shudders were quaking through him. Hysteria or maybe shock.

Other images came to Grey, unbidden. An angry crowd, their gaze sliding away from him as he passed. The man in the transport bay rolling his eyes at Grey's utter ineptitude. The hissed whispers: *Rainy. Earth killing savage.* The words washed over him like ice. He thought of his palms landing painfully on the grit of the transport floor that morning. He thought of all of this happening to Mish.

Grey settled, drawing his shaking hands away from his face. He shook himself violently to clear his head. He wasn't thinking straight. The stress of the journey to Arcanum was colouring his feelings about his wealth. This money was everything to him - to Mish, who had so generously gambled her credits to buy him this chance.

"What happens now?" he asked, his voice steady once again.

*

Xander left Grey in a contemplative daze while he went to retrieve a colleague. Grey spent the time counting his breath and staring at his hands. They were familiar to him, rougher now than they had been in his former life but sprayed with the same freckles and scars he remembered from his youth.

"Hello, Mr. Wright," A woman entered the office with Xander following close behind. She was tall with a serious face and dark cropped hair. She offered a slender hand to him, which he shook. She had a surprisingly strong grip.

"This is Ashby Salinger," said Xander. "She is one of Arcanum Bank's dedicated financial advisors. I thought she might be able to explain your options better."

Grey nodded in greeting, not trusting his voice.

"The first thing we need to do is secure your assets," said Ashby in a clipped voice. Grey got the immediate impression that she was somebody with little tolerance for nonsense. He looked down at her feet to confirm she wasn't a floating robot. "We've found and verified your account and moved your access details to our database on the New Web. Evidence of your liquid assets have been downloaded into this," she presented him with a narrow black box. Inside was an object that reminded Grey of the old stamps they used to use in libraries back when he was in school.

"What is it?" he asked dazedly.

"Microchip," said Ashby. "We've encrypted it and layered in all manners of security to ensure that you and you alone have access to your funds at all times. It'll also ensure that your assets are converted to whatever currency is needed at the point of exchange. For example, when you go to clear your debt with MerryCom, it'll exchange your Arcanum into Ark Credits."

"It gets implanted in your palm," said Xander, helpfully.

"Yes," said Ashby. "Virtually painless and endlessly secure."

"Great," said Grey, trying his best to feign enthusiasm. Grey knew that he had every reason to be dancing with joy at his prospects, but he felt strangely distant from it all. Ashby placed the stamp in his palm and pressed a button. There was a sharp pinching sensation, but Grey didn't flinch. When it was done his palm looked untouched, though he could just barely feel a lump under the skin when he pressed down on the injection site.

"Congratulations, Mr. Wright," said Ashby, her mouth turning up into a smile. The expression made her look much younger. "Welcome to the top fraction of a percentile of wealth,"

"What you might have called… a billionaire?" joked Xander.

Grey pulled his sleeve over his palm, suddenly feeling rather self-conscious. He was no stranger to wealth given his success in his former life, but the enormity of the currency available to him now would have given anybody pause. It was more money than he or his father could have ever imagined for him.

"Thank you, Ms. Salinger," he said.

"Please, call me Ashby," she said. Her demeanour was much warmer towards him now he had what equated to the gross domestic product of a small country embedded in his palm. Xander watched the entire exchange with a look of fascination. Grey supposed that in many ways Xander was watching history in the making.

"What happens next?" asked Grey after a long pause.

"Now that your funds are secure, if you'd like to follow me to the top floor I can set you up with an escort to assist you in closing your

MerryCom account. Once that's in order we'll take you to the leasing office and get you set up with accommodation," Ashby tucked the stamp shaped object back into its box, then slid the box into her pocket. "Generally, houses are placed based on need, but you'll most certainly have your pick of locations. With wealth like that you'll have your pick of most anything from here on out."

"Extraordinary," said Xander under his breath. Ashby raised one critical eyebrow, obviously having heard him.

"We'll get you set up with a transition specialist as well," she said, taking control of the conversation once more. "Somebody to help you adjust to the new world. Think of them as a sort of tutor. They'll catch you up to speed on politics, social issues, things like that. They can help you find a Purpose. If you're interested in working at all, that is,"

Earth killing savage.

"Wait," said Grey. Ashby and Xander, having already started toward the door, turned back to him. "I need a minute. To think."

Ashby blinked at him in surprise. "Of course," she said. "We can step out into the hall,"

"More than that," he interrupted, his voice stronger. "I need-,"

Mish. He needed Mish. It was too much. It was happening too fast. He should have been ecstatic. But there was a wrench in his stomach at the idea of not only facing the hatred of the people outside but joining their ranks. Only he wouldn't be joining. He was a Rainy. Somehow he doubted his economic prowess was going to erase that fact in their minds.

"I need to go home. Back to MerryCom, I mean," he said. "I need to gather my thoughts. Come up with a plan. This is happening so fast."

Xander gaped at him as if he had sprouted a second head. Grey felt his face get hot, sure that Xander thought he was being ungrateful. He wasn't ungrateful at all, just overwhelmed.

Ashby recovered first, her face melting into a professional smile.

"Certainly, Mr. Wright," she said smoothly. "You're the boss."

"Thank you," said Grey, feeling a rush of relief at the prospect of returning to the comforting familiarity of his dorm. He would find Mish and explain everything: the hostility they would face if they decided to leave MerryCom, how inept they'd feel trying to do anything. Mish, trying to find a job in this new world? She'd insist on working. They would still have to do the equivalent of learning a language from scratch. "Please keep this between us for the time being." Said Grey.

"Our confidentiality is assured," said Ashby.

Xander offered to escort Grey back to the transport bay and Grey accepted eagerly. His tablet told him he was a little over an hour away from missing curfew - just enough time to ride the transport back to MerryCom.

The streets were calmer at this time. Grey figured most people were tucked into their homes and eating dinner with their families. It was for the best. Grey didn't know if he could face the hostility again. They walked in near-silence and the trip took half the time with Xander acting as his competent guide. Grey climbed onto the transport, turning back to spare a tiny wave for Xander who waved back, still looking as shell-shocked as earlier.

Grey took a seat nearest to the translucent wall and spent the trip staring at the wilderness slipping by. He rubbed his palm, an echo of Mish's touch, seeking those comforting circles but feeling only the chip in his palm and the uncomfortable weight of getting everything he'd ever thought he wanted.

THIRTEEN

Mish wasn't waiting for Grey when he got back. He asked after her as soon as he reached the MerryCom transportation bay and was told by a gruff guard that she had tried to enter without proper authorisation and was turned away. Grey felt a nervous pang. He didn't like the idea of Mish finding herself on the wrong side of the guards. The same dripping disdain he had met in the streets of the city echoed in the guard's voice. Grey wondered how he had missed it before. He stared at his reflection in the guard's helmet, wild-eyed and wary. Somewhere in between the city and his trek up the mountain he had shifted from overwhelmed to exhausted. Part of him would have liked nothing more than to take his mood out on the guard. To utilise some of his newly gained power to wipe that snide condescension out of the guard's voice. Instead, he adjusted his pack on his shoulder and made his way to the facility.

Mish's room was empty when he arrived, and Grey's stomach sank with disappointment. It struck him as odd. They had spent most of their time together in her room rather than his, so why would she go there now? Unless her dust-up with the transport guards had been more contentious than he had guessed.

He could smell her perfume - that distinct flowery scent that he only associated with her - and he took a moment to breathe in the comfort of it. Nothing was going to make sense to him until he had her in his arms, but being in the familiar comfort of her room, inches from the bed, he was growing more and more accustomed to the thought that waking with her was enough. He wanted to tangle them together in the bed and then he would whisper the day's events in the secret space they created. A small fortress built of their bodies and a blanket. Maybe she had craved being surrounded by him the same way he drew comfort from being in her space. He moved back out to the hallway. He needed the real thing.

Outside his own door he hesitated. His feet felt leaden and clumsy, his limbs weighted and unwilling to move for a moment. Grey shook his head, wondering what was wrong with him. After a day of longing to be with her, suddenly Mish being on the other side of that door was terrifying. Her gamble had paid off and everything was going to change.

Mish was pacing the room when he opened the door, her head jerking towards him as he entered. She threw herself at him and he caught her around the waist, clutching her closely to him and feeling the tension in his body melt away at once. He breathed in the smell of her shampoo, of her skin, and felt a warm rush of emotion blossom in his chest.

"I couldn't eat," her voice was muffled where her lips pressed against his shoulder. "I came straight here after the guard turned me away. I didn't want to miss you."

Grey tangled his hand in her hair and drew her away from him so he could see her. She was trembling all over and her eyes were large and luminous in the dim light. Grey couldn't breathe for a moment. She was the most beautiful thing he had ever seen. He kissed her and she clung to him, her nails digging into his waist when he crushed them together.

"I love you," he said when they broke apart and it sounded like an apology. "I didn't say it before, but - I just love you,"

His voice was hesitant, and his eyes were embarrassingly damp. He hid his outpouring of emotion in her hair, resting his chin on the top of her shoulder. The relief of this homecoming was a stark contrast to his experience outside of the facility. A puzzle piece was clicking into place and with it came a horrible understanding.

"I love you too," she breathed, her body still tight with tension. "But I swear I'm going to be sick if you don't tell me what happened."

And there it was. The reality of the choice some part of him had made the moment Xander read him the balance of his account. Before that - maybe while he stood in the street covered in spit and surrounded by the resentful Proto whispers. Maybe even before he climbed onto the transport that morning.

Earth killing savage.

It's so hollow.

The world was too big and too unpredictable, and Grey realised in that moment that Mish was never going to understand. How could he protect her and protect the fragile, simple, beautiful life they were building together if they lived in a society they didn't understand, surrounded by people who felt nothing but resentment toward them? What happened when it was Mish who was spat on? Berated? Or worse. And he, in all his ineptitude, worth nothing outside of the currency in his account, a useless dullard who couldn't even read the signs on the street. A life that would get infinitely more complex, with more choices, more plans to make and experiences to chase. How could their simple bliss survive out there?

He couldn't tell her the truth, not when the stakes were so high. She would try to convince him that they could make it work. She wouldn't believe that money would fail to insulate them from the hate. If she believed in the hate at all. He couldn't let her choose because he knew she would choose wrong. He needed more time to think this through, to formulate a plan.

Mish seemed to read something in his expression, and she pulled away from him, covering her mouth with her hands and backing away with wide eyes. She didn't speak. Even with her preternatural understanding, Grey knew he was going to have to say it. He swallowed the lump in his throat.

"I couldn't access it," he said, eyes trained on her face. "There is no money," Her face crumpled, and Grey felt it like a physical blow, but he didn't look away. He would take in every second of her heartbreak as penance for the lie. He deserved it. Probably deserved worse.

For all of her obvious heartbreak, Mish didn't cry. She sank onto his bed, her face smoothing into an unreadable mask as she stared, unseeing, at the opposite wall. Grey sat next to her, hating his own cowardice.

"I'm sorry," he said, truly meaning the words. "Mish, I'm so sorry."

"I can't-," her voice cracked, and she stopped, taking in a deep, juddering breath. "Tomorrow," she said as she composed herself. "I need...," she trailed off and then laid down, curling her legs up to her chest and turning to face the wall.

Grey placed a hand on her back, feeling the ridges of her spine under his splayed fingers. Slow and soft, her breathing calmed after a while as she slipped into some fitful place between awake and asleep. Finally, he curled next to her, wrapping her in his arms and making silent promises in his head that he was doing the right thing.

After a while Grey slipped into a restless sort of sleep, never entirely losing his awareness of Mish's weight beside him. Even with her tossing and turning beside him, the guilt wasn't enough to outweigh the relief he felt at holding her. The absolute joy of lying with her in the cocoon of his room, knowing that in a couple of hours they would wake, work, and do it all over again. The predictable routine that spelt out hundreds of delectably safe days that stretched ahead of them as far as he could see.

Mish shifted in the darkness and something about her stillness told Grey that she was awake. He roused himself to consciousness with the slip of her skin under his fingers as he stroked the length of her arm. There was something impossibly vulnerable about her just then, hidden in the darkness, only real where he touched her - something delicate and beautiful and raw in how they came together in silence.

"Sometimes I think we're like Sisyphus," said Grey in a low voice.

Mish didn't answer, but he could tell she was listening by the way her hands stilled on his chest.

"Do you remember Sisyphus?" Grey paused, allowing her space to answer, and barrelling forward when she didn't. "He was a king of Corinth who cheated death twice. He tricked Hades and his wife, Persephone, to escape the underworld. After that, the Gods let him live out the remainder of his natural life. But, when he finally died, Zeus set him an impossible task. He was to push a boulder endlessly up a hill only to have it roll back down to the bottom before he reached the crest. For eternity,"

"You think we're cursed," said Mish, her soft voice muffled against his chest.

"Cursed?" asked Grey, puzzled. "You think Zeus cursed him?"

"You don't?" Mish's weight shifted in the darkness and he could sense her hovering somewhere above him. "A pointless task for him to repeat until the end of time? And for what? Taking an opportunity to live again?"

Grey bit his lip. "I think it was a lesson," he said carefully. "Sisyphus spent his life scheming and plotting to escape his fate, so Zeus set out to teach him hubris. Maybe to find meaning in the repetition. An impossible task, sure, but not a curse. Not really. There are moments of beauty in it, aren't there?"

Moments like this. The two of them tucked safely together.

Grey knew Mish had to understand it on some level. She, with her eternal understanding and unflinching optimism, had to see the good in their lives now.

"He was nothing more than a slave for the Gods to laugh at," Mish bit out, her voice startlingly cold. "I bet he'd rather be dead. I know I would."

Would? Or do? Thought Grey, but he couldn't bring himself to say it out loud. The answer and the question were both too horrible to contemplate. He felt her weight shift as she laid down beside him once more, only this time he didn't reach for her. The guilt was welling up inside of him, shaken loose by the onslaught of her anger. How could he possibly deserve to touch her now? It would be a selfish comfort only to him.

There was a heartbeat where he almost told her. His tongue perched behind his lips, ready to explain, to grovel, anything that would make her understand.

Instead, he lay until the edges of his room began to glow with the beginning kiss of dawn, counting Mish's breaths, and praying to any Gods who might be listening that she might forgive him when he finally told her the truth - three years of her life, gone.

FOURTEEN

On the day that changed everything, Mish woke like she had every day since the failed Arcanum experiment.

She heard the chimes but stayed perfectly still, her eyes shut against the morning until she felt Grey shift awake beside her. She kept her breath low and even, willing herself to stillness when she felt the brush of his lips on her forehead. She continued the charade until she heard the shower tube slide closed and then exhaled a sigh of relief.

It had been six weeks since Grey's attempted recovery of his account and Mish still couldn't bear letting him see her during these broken moments in the morning. Moments she checked her Chroniker with the obsession of a drug addict and bit her knuckles with frustration when it continued to tick the days away just one by one by one. Mish didn't know what she expected to see - maybe a glitch that would return her hundreds of credits? Some programming bug that would take pity on her and her bad decisions? It was those moments, raw knuckles tucked under her thighs to save them from her abuse, that she thought of her father. How many times had she watched him throw his life away on a random chance? How could she have been so stupid as to fall into the same sickness? When she looked in the mirror, she felt the same revulsion as she'd felt watching him sob on that stoop.

Mish needed these early morning moments alone to collect her broken pieces before she could interact with Grey. If he had any idea how distraught she really was he would be overcome with guilt. So, she bandaged her bloody fingers and observed the stillness in her room, wrapping it around herself until her shoulders steadied and she felt ready to face the day. 'Steady' was as close to 'happy' as she could manage those days.

For his part, Grey was unfailingly supportive. They fell into a strained routine following his return from the city with Grey tiptoeing around her black dog moods and holding her when she cried quietly throughout the night. Mish knew she was being unfair to him, he had only done what she asked of him after all, but a dark, nasty part of her wondered how hard he had really tried. He'd been so hesitant to accept the day pass. Maybe Mish should have gone with him - but that would have been impossible. She barely had enough credits for one of them to go. Mish trusted Grey. And she loved Grey. Loved his bedhead and his sense of humour. Loved the way she could see his mind working, constantly categorising, and planning his next move. She needed to keep the self-loathing she felt from poisoning her against him.

By the time Grey finished his shower, Mish was up and dressed, tying her hair into a knot at the nape of her neck.

"Good morning," Mish said, trying to mimic her normal morning charm. Her voice sounded flat in her own ears, but Grey either didn't notice or decided not to acknowledge it.

"Hey, you," Grey said. He drew her to him, wrapping his arms around her waist, pulling her back against his chest. Mish melted into the embrace, taking a moment of solace to lay her head back and listen to his even breaths.

"How did you sleep?" he asked, kissing her cheek.

"Fine," Mish lied. Moving away from the warmth of Grey's body was excruciating, so she turned to kiss him instead. Kissing Grey was like taking a deep breath after spending a long time underwater. She inhaled him, swallowed his breath as she ran her hands under his shirt, revelling in the joy she only seemed to feel when they were connecting like this. They shifted and she felt the cool surface of the wall at her back.

The sound of chimes broke through.

"That's the alarm," Grey said. "We'll be late."

"Let's be late," Mish breathed, kissing the spot on his neck that made his fingers twitch on her waist.

"Mish-," Grey stepped away, breaking their contact.

It was like being plunged back under the dark water of her shame and grief. Mish felt a wave of resentment she knew was completely unwarranted. She clenched her hands into fists, struggling for composure. Her emotions varied wildly since Grey's return. Near-catatonic episodes punctuated with explosive anger or infinite sadness.

Finally, her heart rate slowed. She retrieved her shoes and sat on the bed to lace them up.

"Have you-," Grey paused, running a nervous hand through his hair. Mish watched him from the corner of her eye but kept her focus on the laces. "Have you ever thought about kids?"

Mish tightened the double knot and pushed off of the bed. "What about them?"

Grey was nervous, bouncing from foot to foot and unable to meet her eyes.

"I just…do you want them?" he asked, voice soft.

Mish was collecting her things for the workday. She was assigned janitorial duties in the Proto canteen, which meant gloves, hat, boots-

"Mish?" Grey said.

"What?" she asked, pulling on her hat.

"Do you want kids?" he asked again.

"I don't know," she shrugged, spinning the disk to open the door.

"Oh," the disappointment in Grey's voice was palpable. "Because I - when I was out there, I was imagining what it would be like - how we would live and I thought maybe-,"

"No point talking about it when we've both got about," Mish checked her Chroniker. "Ten and a half years of servitude left."

Grey's features crystallised into an unreadable mask. Mish felt a pang. Once again, she was failing in her quest to assuage his guilt. Part of her didn't care, though. She wished for a moment that he would shout at her. Call her a brat. Give her the punishment she craved as an escape from beating herself up.

Grey just finished pulling on his uniform with careful movements, not looking at her. Mish turned on her heel and stomped down the hallway, sure that Grey would catch up any moment with those long legs of his. But he kept his distance until they reached check-in at the break room. Then, he snuck her a small hug so sweetly that Mish felt a ripple of regret. But the guilt didn't last. Deep underneath the glassy surface of her emotions was anger. How could he talk to her about children as if they had any semblance of a real future?

*

Scrubbing the canteen clean was an excellent distraction from Mish's dark mood. Repetition didn't appeal to her the way it did to Grey. Mish much preferred the tasks with a clear positive outcome. Mopping the floors until they shone like glass, polishing the buffet table to a new metal sheen, repairing chipped sealant on the dining tables, those were the tasks that Mish could lose herself in. Mind-numbing steps culminating into changes she could see. The only danger was getting lost in her thoughts.

"Alright, Mish?" It was Cherry, prepping the buffet for lunch service while Mish cleaned the grout surrounding the dish tank.

Mish unclenched her jaw, surprised at the aching sensation. "Living the dream."

"Which dream? You dream about the dish tank?" asked Cherry and Mish struggled not to roll her eyes.

"It's just a saying, Cherry," said Mish. Cherry was vitrified in the late 2200s and they often didn't understand each other's phrasing. "It means I'm doing fine."

"Oh. Good," Cherry slid a dish of hot toasted sandwiches onto the buffet and smiled sweetly at Mish. Mish smiled back out of habit.

"How are you?" she asked, hoping that Cherry would launch into a long story that Mish only had to half-listen to.

"Living the dream," Cherry said, her smile widening.

This time Mish's smile was genuine. "I'm sorry," she said. "It's been a long day so far."

Cherry bit her lip and leaned close. With her wide blue eyes and golden hair, she reminded Mish of the princesses in stories of her first life. Once upon a time, Mish might have been jealous of her effortless beauty.

"I saw you checking that," Cherry said, gesturing to Mish's Chroniker.

Mish covered the face of the band with her hand, hoping Cherry hadn't seen her dismal balance.

"Please don't be embarrassed," said Cherry. "The tunnel is just as long in the middle,"

It was another unfamiliar phrase, but Mish thought she could parse out Cherry's meaning this time. She lowered her grout brush and wiped the sweat from her forehead.

"It has been hard lately. I made a - well, a bad bet," said Mish. "That might be slang, er, a gamble?"

Cherry's mouth quirked up. "Had some of those in my time,"

"Well, this one went badly. All of this trouble for a second life and I'll have wasted half of mine in this facility," Mish's voice trembled, and she bit the inside of her cheek. She was not going to cry. If she started now, she wouldn't stop.

Cherry placed a soft hand on Mish's.

"Have you thought about speeding it up?" Cherry said so quietly that Mish could barely hear her over the hum of the dishwasher.

Mish glanced around the room, her gaze lingering on the guards posted at the door. There was a rumour that the guards had listening devices in their helmets to keep tabs on Rainy conversations. Mish had never put much stock in rumours, but if Cherry was talking about what she thought she was… it was better to be safe than sorry.

"How?" asked Mish in a low voice.

"There's the usual way," said Cherry.

Mish blanched. She had always approached her time at MerryCom with the same diligence she exercised in her first life. She kept her head down and did her work as expected. But that didn't mean she was naive. There was an entire subculture of seedy commerce playing out in the Rainy population. Trading credits for better rooms, better shifts, clothing, rations-anything that could be useful during their stay was game. Mish had always stayed out of it. There were too many ways for a woman to be exploited there.

"I couldn't do that," she said, certain that Cherry wasn't talking about taking on extra shifts for credits. Sex was as much a commodity as anything else at MerryCom. But the trade wasn't something Mish or most of the people she associated with would have participated in. Unless Cherry had? "I've nothing against people who do, but I, I just couldn't."

"You don't have to do all that," said Cherry kindly. "I wouldn't recommend it anyway. The guards don't like it."

Both women shot nervous glances at the guards. Then Cherry whispered in Mish's ear:

"Actually, I'm told some of them *do*. But they'd never admit it. Not with a Rainy, anyhow."

"I suppose not," said Mish shakily. "But still-,"

"But of course, you can't. Grey. I understand," said Cherry. "But maybe you get close to someone who has been here a long time, like your supervisor? They can... tip you, you know. From their own balance. For good work."

"Can they?" Mish struggled to keep her voice light. Had there been a whole micro-economy going on around her the whole time, while she'd had her head down, buffing tables? Her heart was galloping in her chest and she turned back to the grout so Cherry wouldn't see the feverish excitement lighting up her eyes. "What does good work entail?"

"In my experience?" Cherry raised a mischievous eyebrow. "Like a beautiful girl paying just a little extra attention. You don't have to do anything, just give the impression that you could, then ask for a little bonus for your company,"

Mish tightened her jaw once more and the muscles started to feel rubbery and swollen. "It's that easy, huh?"

"It can be," said Cherry. "For us,"

Mish was surprised to hear Cherry mark them as equals. She had never considered herself vain before, but the idea of using her beauty to exercise some control in this uncontrollable situation was stirring. Still, she wondered about Cherry's motives in telling her about the possibility of getting tipped. Labour and Maintenance's closest thing to a supervisor was-

"But Cherry, my supervisor is sort of…well, it's Mark. Surely you wouldn't want me getting overly friendly with him?"

Cherry tipped her head to one shoulder, kind of like a shrug "But anyway, there are others. Teams outside Labour and Maintenance. Opportunities to mingle."

Mish lowered the grout brush once more.

"I need to think about it," she said. "Please don't say anything to the others."

"I wouldn't," said Cherry. "They don't understand. It's different for us," she sounded very tired then and Mish felt a pang of emotion. Cherry was so quick and perceptive, looking after Mish when it hadn't even occurred to her to do the same.

"Move it along," a guard barked into the canteen, sending Mish and Cherry both jumping back to their tasks.

*

Cherry's suggestion occupied Mish's thoughts through the rest of the first shift and into the lunch break. She chewed her sandwich, lost in the possibilities, while Grey and the others came to join her and began their boisterous conversation. Mish tried to smile and nod at the right times, but her eyes were scouring the canteen, sizing up other Rainies and wondering who was wealthy enough to tip. Who had more power? Shift supervisors at

Hydroponics? The Engineers, who did the maintenance tasks that were too important for Maintenance? It was almost fun, almost like she was playacting as a spy, seeking out her mark. Nothing was going to come of it, so what was the harm in speculating?

"Saint Mish is lost in the clouds," said Mark with a jovial laugh. Mish blinked, dragging her attention back to the table guiltily.

"Sorry," she swallowed. "Haven't been sleeping much," Grey slung his arm around her chair, gently rubbing her neck with one hand.

"That's shit," said Troy. "Actually, I was thinking about splurging on a Booster. Do you want a sip?"

"That's alright. They hurt my stomach," said Mish, thinking of the syrupy thickness of the drink. It only cost a fraction of a credit, but Mish couldn't stomach even that charity.

"Suit yourself," he said, scraping his chair back so it squealed against Mish's newly polished floors.

"I'll get it," said Mark. "I owe you from last week."

Mish's gaze followed him as he crossed the canteen to the vending units against the wall until she caught Cherry's eye. She flushed, embarrassed, knowing that Cherry would assume she was considering pressing Mark for a tip. But Cherry only nodded at Mish, a gesture that plainly read *go for it*.

"I'll be right back," she said before she could lose her nerve. She picked her way through the lunch crowd, reaching the vending unit just as Mark was lifting his arm to scan his Chroniker. And just then, the display tilted up, giving her a glimpse-

Mish gasped.

Mark spun on his heel at the sound. Mish knew she should compose her expression, walk away, do anything to hide the enormity of the number she had seen, but she couldn't do it. The figure was so large.

She was trembling with the discovery, her mind whirling so fast that thoughts slipped away from her like oil on water.

Mark scowled.

"A word, Mish?" and he led her out of the canteen and into the hallway. Mish tried to keep down the hysterical bubble that was building in her chest.

"What did you think you were doing?" Mark asked darkly, as they rounded the corner into an empty hallway.

"I, I didn't-,"

"Yes, you did," he said coldly. "I saw you peek at it."

Mish hung her head, unable to meet his eyes. "I'm sorry, it was an accident, I," the lie caught between her teeth.

Mark ran a hand over his face, ruffled his own hair. "Do you understand what an invasion of privacy this is?" he asked. "There's a reason we don't display our balances, Mish."

"Why do you have a balance at all?" The question slipped out before Mish could stop it.

"That's none of your business."

"Mark, you can pay your carbon tax several times over with those credits,"

"You don't know what you're talking about," Mark snapped. His voice was quiet, but his breath was panicked and raspy. He broke away from her, his hands roughing through his hair. Mish didn't think she'd ever seen him as distressed as this.

"Hey," she said, low and quiet, the way she used to coach her clients through panic attacks. "Mark, hey. I'm sorry, okay? You're right. It's none of my business. I won't say anything."

He didn't speak, but the tension in his shoulders loosened.

"You don't have to tell me why. I won't say anything," she said again in that same low voice. She took a step closer and placed a gentle hand on his forearm. The gesture was intended to be friendly, but Mark stilled at her touch, his gaze falling to just above his Chroniker, where her hand rested against his skin. Mish felt a strange thrill at the proximity. She took another cautious step forward, bit her lip, close enough now that she had to look up to see Mark's eyes. He covered her hand with his.

"Are you joking with this?" he said, his voice completely devoid of his usual humour. "Are you fucking kidding me right now?"

Mish stumbled back. He was *laughing* at her. Humourless laughter and cruel eyes.

"I'm not doing anything," she snapped, humiliation shooting up her spine, heating every inch of her skin.

"Bullshit, Mish. Have you been talking to Cherry? This is her sort of side hustle, isn't it? Don't think I don't know what she's doing, Mish. I'm not an idiot" There was anger, real anger in Mark's eyes. "Didn't have you down as playing this sort of game, though. How many departments are you sneaking around to, batting your eyelashes? Does Grey know?"

"It's not-," Mish tried to choke out, but she couldn't speak. Humiliated tears sprang to her eyes and a lump was caught in her throat so tightly that she could barely breathe. She couldn't defend herself, not when he was so blatantly right.

"Get out of here," Mark snapped. "If you tell anybody what you saw I'll have the guards penalise you, I swear I will."

Mish didn't need to be told twice. She turned and raced down the empty hall, collapsing against the wall as soon as she was out of earshot. There was pressure building behind her eyes and her head pounded. She tore the bandage off her knuckle, biting down until she could taste blood and pain replaced her humiliation.

Footsteps were echoing down the hallway and for one terrible moment Mish wondered if Mark had changed his mind and sent the guards after all. But it was only Grey, rounding the corner looking so concerned that Mish started sobbing all over again.

"Are you okay?" he asked, pulling her to him. "Mark said you were sick - what did you do to your hand?"

Mish glanced down at her bloody fingers and swallowed hard.

"I'm not sick," she said. "I caught my hand in the vending unit, is all."

"Oh, Mish," said Grey, wrapping her in a tight embrace. This time Mish couldn't melt into it. Her skin prickled with the contact. She could still her hand on Mark's arm, still feel the madness that had made her reach for him and it sickened her. He would tell Grey eventually. It was only a matter of time. Sending him her way was a kindness, an opportunity for her to come clean on her own, but Mark would tell someday, and she would finally lose this special bond that she had spent weeks pushing away.

"I need to go to the med centre," she said, pushing past him.

"Of course," Grey said. "I'll walk you."

Mish winced, being careful not to let him touch her again. She was sure he would smell the guilt on her somehow.

"I was thinking, hey, would you slow down?" Grey jogged a couple of steps to catch up to her. "Let's have a date tonight."

"A date?" Mish asked. The possibility of something new - a change in the routine.

"We can't go anywhere, yeah, but we could have a picnic in the room," he said. "Just you and me,"

"I don't want a damn picnic," Mish snapped. "And don't look at me like that."

Grey's face changed, an attempt to hide his concern. His compliance only made Mish angrier. His thoughtful consideration of her feelings made the guilt worse. She was going to suffer under the weight of it.

"You need to stop trying to make me happy here," she said. "You have to let me feel the way I feel about this place."

"Mish," Grey reached for her, but stopped himself. "I need to tell you something,"

"What?" she asked.

Grey's eyes darted from her face to her bloody knuckle and back again. "I know this has been hard for you,"

Mish turned and walked away. She couldn't listen to another one of his speeches, couldn't stomach him being so kind and supportive knowing that he would never look at her the same way once Mark told him what she tried to do. Grey didn't follow her this time, which was lucky because she didn't want to go to the med centre at all.

There was a rage building in her, burning through her limbs until they moved of their own accord. The injustice of her life was too much to handle, so she gave over to her body's impulses. A weight settled in her chest and with it came a plan. A terrible, desperate plan.

She found herself in the janitor's closet, hand wrapped around the handle of a mop while she stared at the glass screen of the information monitor. Intended for new Rainies to research cleaning protocols, the monitor was useless to her this far into her sentence and its cheerful touch screen was infuriating. Mish lifted the mop and swung at the glass with a feral scream. Her reward was the spiderweb cracks in the glass.

Mish swung again. And again. Again. Until the screen went black, and shards of glass littered the floor. An alarm screamed in the distance, but Mish was preoccupied with the satisfaction of pouring her anger into destruction. She stopped, listening to the sounds of the guard's footsteps as they raced towards the closet. They would reach her soon. There wasn't much time left.

She placed the mop in its spot on the wall, careful not to displace any other cleaning instruments. The glass sparkled up like precious jewels below her and she knelt, sifting through the pieces until she found one of the appropriate size. Having selected the perfect shard, she slipped it into her waistband and turned to face the door, ready for whatever the guards had in store for her.

FIFTEEN

"Would you say that you anticipate another 'difficult day'?" the counsellor leaned forward, the first indication that she had been listening to Mish's explanation of her behaviour. When the guards led her out of the closet with the promise of a psychiatric evaluation, Mish had pictured something more personal. Instead, the counsellor asked her basic questions about which events led to what and took notes on her tablet. Mish suspected these questions had more to do with filling in an incident report than getting to the bottom of Mish's emotional torment.

"Definitely not. No more difficult days," said Mish, hands clasped in her lap. "It was completely out of character for me. I'm not prone to outbursts."

"I believe that," said the counsellor, lounging comfortably in her chair once more. "We expect the occasional tantrum from our Rainies. The majority of you were affluent enough to afford the procedure. Shifting to the labour force, well, it is a difficult adjustment."

Mish bristled at the word *'tantrum'*. Like she was a toddler screaming just to hear her own voice rather than a grown woman trapped in a world where she had no options. She grit her teeth.

"That's almost certainly it," she said, and her words were acid, burning her throat on the way out. "It all got to be too much today. When the monitor stopped working I lost my temper."

There was a long pause while the counsellor tapped away. After a while Mish wondered if she'd forgotten about her completely. Should she stand? Mish was pretty sure she was supposed to wait to be dismissed.

"I see in your file that you worked in the social sector in your proto life?" asked the counsellor.

"I did, yes."

The counsellor nodded, her focus shifting back to the tablet in her hand. "Normally in these situations we mandate two follow up evaluations. Standard practice to avoid any more incidents with company property,"

Mish wondered if 'company property' meant the information monitor or her. Maybe both.

"But, considering your familiarity with similar therapeutic processes, I am content to release you without restrictions."

"Thank you," said Mish.

The counsellor's eyes flicked up from her tablet and met Mish's. "Please understand that this is merely a professional courtesy and you will remain under close scrutiny by the guards. Should you make a spectacle of yourself in the future, the situation will change."

"I understand. It won't happen again."

"See that it doesn't," said the counsellor, waving Mish off at last.

Mish turned out of the counsellor's doorway and found herself nearly walking into the uniformed chest of a masked guard. She blinked her shock away. It made sense that they would assign her an escort. They could hardly let a violent Rainy roam free in the facility.

"Hello," she said, looking upwards into the reflective mask cautiously.

The guard turned on their heel in response and began leading the way back to the dormitories. Mish followed, keeping her head down as they passed other groups of Rainies. There was little entertainment at MerryCom. Mish was certain the whole compound would have heard of her exploits by now.

"It's to the left, actually," said Mish when they reached a fork in the hallway. "I'm cohabitating." *For however long that lasts.*

The guard gestured for her to take the lead and she did, limbs shaking as they approached the correct door. Everything was riding on the conversation she would have on the other side of that door. If she could make him understand - if he didn't kick her out immediately, she was sure she could set things straight.

Mark opened the door looking equally sleepy and confused to see Mish standing there, her guard posted in the hall behind her. Mish was trembling all over. All Mark would have to do was ask her what the hell she was doing there and the guard would drag her off. Mish hadn't known what the counsellor meant by 'restrictions' but she had a hunch it was more than reduced alcohol rations.

"Forgot my key," Mish said, her voice hoarse with anxiety, her eyes pleading with Mark.

He considered her for half of a beat too long, eyes not quite narrowing but far from friendly before stepping aside. "Of course," he allowed her into the room, pausing to shoot the guard a genial wave.

Mish stepped into the space, wiping her clammy hands on her uniform, suddenly overcome with the urge to shrink herself into invisibility.

"What are you doing here, Mish?" Mark asked once the door had closed and they were alone.

"I'm here to apologise," said Mish. "Properly this time."

Mark ran a hand over his face, his frustration palpable. "The guard will be gone by now. You should go," He reached for the door.

"Please don't," said Mish, her voice wavering. "Please, Mark. I'm absolutely sick at how I behaved."

His hand stilled before it reached the disk and he considered her, his eyes skating softly over her features the way he had noticed before and chosen to ignore.

"I'm not going to tell Grey," said Mark, his voice softer this time. "You don't have to worry."

"I'm not worried about Grey," Mish tilted her head, letting her hair spill over her shoulders like a cascade of silk. "It's your opinion I care about."

"Stop that," said Mark. His jaw was tight, but he didn't move when Mish took one slow step closer.

"Stop what?"

"I know what you're doing," he said, but his eyes were caught somewhere near her mouth.

"How could you?" she asked. "When I don't," She was a breath away now, her hands resting on the planes of his chest.

"Dammit, Mish," Mark growled, jerking his chin away from her and up to the ceiling.

A wild desperation overtook her then. She snaked her arms around his neck and pulled herself closer, anything she could to recapture the moment.

"Stop, Mish, please, *stop*," Mark pulled her arms away from him and stepped out of the embrace. "I know you don't really want this."

Mish stepped back, dizzy. She had been so certain that she had already lost all of her dignity that afternoon, but this humiliation was just as potent. The rejection was so shocking. It was as if somebody had poured a bucket of ice water down her spine. And he was right. She didn't want it, but she needed to be free of MerryCom and she needed somebody to see that.

"Mish," Mark said, more kindly than she had ever heard from him. "Can you tell me what's going on?"

Mish shook her head.

"Please," he said again. "Can we just talk?"

Mark stepped away from her slowly, as if she were a skittish animal, looked at his bed, and seemed to think better of it. He spun the chair away from his desk and sat gingerly, his eyes finding Mish once more.

He could have called for the guards, thought Mish, *but he didn't. Nothing is irreparable here.*

Not that she really believed that. It was an old adage that she used to give her clients when situations seemed especially dire. Back when Mish could see above the surface of the water. Back when problems were waves to be endured.

"I'm sorry," she said for what seemed like the millionth time that day. "I don't know what's come over me."

Mark surveyed her steadily, considering. "Grey told me you've had some troubles."

Mish snorted, feeling that awful lurch of resentments that so often accompanied her thoughts of Grey. "You could say that." She wasn't going to elaborate on that, and the silence stretched uncomfortably between them.

"I suppose that you have questions about my-," said Mark after a while. He was fidgeting again, his knee bouncing up and down. "Well, you know. It's just… I really can't have you telling people. I'm hoping we can agree on that?"

Mish's jaw was sore again. She was beginning to worry for her teeth. This was why he hadn't told Grey, of course, which meant Mish had some small leverage. Another bit of hope.

"I see what you mean," she nodded, her gaze trained on her feet, the picture of contrition. "But I can't say I understand," She heard Mark sigh, but kept her eyes lowered.

"It's difficult to explain if you've never been out," he said. "I have enough to leave, but I'm not sure I want to."

"You can't mean that." said Mish.

"I do, though," he said, shifting in his chair uncomfortably. "I was going to leave. Had it scheduled and everything. When you have enough credits to pay your fine, MerryCom issues a day pass so you can travel to the Reparations Office and then swing by Lodging Assignment to work out your placement. I was supposed to take the day pass and then come back to pay my fine.

"I was excited, Mish. So excited. It felt like I had won the lottery - finally getting to see what the real world looks like—experiencing life as a Proto with all their advancements. I got to the city and it was *incredible*. The buildings, the nature, seeing the world whole again. I vitrified right after the oil wars, you know? I had never seen the sky so blue-," he trailed off, lost somewhere in memory.

"If it was so beautiful, what stopped you from leaving?" asked Mish.

"It wasn't real," said Mark. "The people out there, they hate us. The rebuild wasn't that long ago for them, and it was hard. There was sickness afterwards. Birth defects, mass disabling events, death. Their grandparents, parents even, lost in the effort," he clasped his hands in his lap and shook his head. "That's why they started the reanimations. Imagine an entire generation missing from the workforce. They needed us to fill the gaps. But we were the ones who were wealthy enough to skip ahead, we profited off of murdering the planet that we left for them and they'll never forgive us for it."

Mish shook her head. "It's still got to be better than this. Forced labour, living a life that's not really your own?"

"I promise you, it's not," said Mark, his voice soft and insistent. "And there's more than just the people. MerryCom wants us to believe that the world is this utopian paradise outside of this facility, but that's just the lie they sell us to make us work hard. I wandered around that city for hours, getting pushed, hissed at, spit on - you name it, until I got to the outskirts."

"What did you find?" Mish asked. She watched the muscles of his throat contract as he swallowed, looking a little pale.

"Slums," he said. "Extreme poverty. War. Just like the wars I left when I vitrified. They were carting in Rainies by the busload to fight people out of the city. Keep them at bay,"

"I don't believe you," said Mish. "Just outside the city like that? I doubt they'd let you wander that far."

"It's true, Mish," said Mark. "And I'm not the only one who's seen it. If you really don't believe me, ask Grey," his eyes were hard, and it was Mish's turn to swallow.

She knew Grey had a failed former assignment, but it wasn't something they ever discussed. He had said it was a combat position, but it hadn't lasted long enough for him to figure out his location, and Mish couldn't imagine that their area of paradise was so small. Was it possible that the rebuilding had such narrow reach?

"It doesn't matter," she said finally, slowly shaking her head.

"Doesn't it?" asked Mark. "It does to me. I'm happier here, away from all of the cruelty."

"I'd rather participate in a cruel world with my own choices than play captive to a corporation," said Mish.

"I don't see it that way," said Mark. "I have choices. I chose to stay here. Where I have friends and a job that I'm good at. I've built a comfortable life."

"No," snapped Mish. "You were allowed a safe life in exchange for your captivity. You're a dog, Mark. MerryCom's pet dog."

Mark lifted an eyebrow. "I'm surprised, Mish. I always assumed you thought highly of me."

"How could I?" Mish snapped. "You went out once, got swatted on the nose, and came back with your tail tucked."

"I'm not sure that's fair."

"What's not fair is you sitting on a mountain of credits that you refuse to use."

"I do use them."

"For what?" asked Mish. "Toss a couple Cherry's way so you don't have to sleep alone? Grab Troy a Booster here and there and convince yourself that you're charitable? You're not a 'free spirit', Mark. You're scared. It's pathetic."

"I'm pathetic?" asked Mark, his voice sharper than before. Mish hit some sort of nerve in him. She could tell by his clenched jaw and tight shoulders. The force of his anger lifted him from his chair and sent him pacing across the room. "It's ironic, you bringing up Cherry considering why you came here tonight."

Mish flinched, but quickly recovered. "At least I see the cage for what it is. At least I'm trying to get out,"

"Right, bang up job so far," said Mark with a nasty laugh. "Wasting your credits on a lottery's chance. Really well done,"

"I had to try. If there was a chance to get us out-,"

"And now you're back to square one," Mark said.

"I can't understand it, Mark. I really can't. How can you live like this? Labour, day in and day out,"

"Saint Mish thinks she's too good for labour, does she?"

"That's not what I said," she snapped.

"But it's how you feel. Clearly, since you came here tonight and tried to seduce me out of my credits. Who's really the pathetic one here?"

"You seemed pretty game earlier," said Mish, heart pounding, hand reaching for her back pocket. This was escalating in a way she had hoped to avoid, but she was in too deep now.

Mark surveyed her, eyes practically burning with his frustration. For a wild moment she wondered how she could escalate it further, convince him to hit her, anything to justify what she was about to do.

"Mish," he said in a controlled voice. "This is getting out of hand."

Mish took a step closer. Her legs were weak, but her hands were steady. "What if you gave me your credits?"

Mark stilled then. He eyed her warily. "No, Mish."

"You're not going to use them anyway," she said. "It wouldn't even be your full balance. Just enough to get me out."

"What happened to all of that 'we' talk earlier?" he asked. "Forgotten about Grey already?"

"I'll get him out somehow," said Mish, her stomach lurching queasily. "But I need this."

"It's not going to happen, Mish," said Mark.

"Why not?"

"We don't belong out there," he said. "I know you don't understand, but I'm telling you,"

"Mark," Mish interrupted. "Give me the credits."

"No."

Mish sprang into action with a fluidity that surprised her. One moment she was across the room, and the next she was holding the glass monitor shard to Mark's neck, pressing hard enough to draw a scarlet bead of blood.

"Do it," she growled.

"Don't do this, Mish," Mark said softly. "This is a mistake. This isn't who you are."

"Who I am is none of your business," she increased her pressure and Mark's eyes went wide. There was a rush of pleasure in seeing his fear. "Initiate the transfer."

"Okay, Jesus, okay, I'm doing it," Mark said, reaching a shaking hand for his Chroniker.

There were a series of beeps and then the Chroniker on Mish's wrist vibrated. A small firework projection informed her that her credit debt level had been reached, the celebratory tone seeming macabre while she held Mark hostage.

"Thank you," she said and stepped away from Mark gingerly. "I'm sorry," She backed away towards the door in slow, even steps, worried that he would lunge at her or call the alarm. His hand went to his neck, stemming the thin trickle of blood.

"Please don't do this," he said when she reached the door. "We're friends. I promise we can work this out, Mish, please. You can't come back from something like this."

Mish twisted the disk to open the door, stepping backwards into the doorway.

"Please don't call them," she said softly. "If we're really friends. Please, Mark, I need this."

He looked unbearably sad then and Mish had to turn away to escape her sickening guilt. In the hallway, she dropped the glass and broke into a sprint, silencing her Chroniker along the way, pulling her sleeve over it. Could she trust Mark not to call the guards? She didn't think even their friendship could withstand armed robbery. But all she had to do was reach the ticket office and pay her debt and she would be free.

Finally.

It was late. Too late to reasonably be roaming the halls. Luckily for Mish, the guard who'd escorted her to Mark's room must have assumed it was hers and clocked off for the night. The rest had finished their rounds throughout the dorms and retired to wherever guards got off to when they weren't harassing the Rainies. It was perfect timing, fate, the universe finally working for her.

She was just crossing the breezeway when the first alarm sounded. The blaring drone was loud enough to startle her to a stop, her shoes squealing against the concrete. Mark had called the guards after all. She had no right to feel stung, but it hurt all the same. It took her a heartbeat to recover, but she hurried on.

The world narrowed to the sound of the alarm, the shouts and echoing from halls away, and her destination at the ticket office.

Pay the debt. You'll never see Mark after you pay the debt. They can't touch you once you pay the debt. You're not company property once you pay the debt.

It was a new mantra, and she wasn't sure there was any truth in it. Her brain was sedated by terror and hope, unable to conceive of anything past the next hallway, the next door, the shallow pits of her breath and finally-

"I'm here to pay my debt," she shouted into the ticket office monitor. It was a blessedly automated service and the machine whirred to life without a moment's suspicion for the ringing alarms or her panicked appearance. Voices sounded down the hall, closer and closer still while Mish keyed her information into the monitor. A loading screen appeared, with the details of her life laid out starkly like numbers on a page. Then a red bar reading: SECURITY BREACH.

"No," said Mish, her breath escaping her in a violent rush. She gripped the sides of the monitor until her knuckles were white. "No, no, no, come on, no-," she shook the machine, letting out little hysterical sobs. She had the credits *right there*. She was so *close*.

"Stop right there!"

A thunder of voices as guards streamed into the hall, a sea of shiny helmets and batons waving.

She wished, with a rush of longing so palpable that it was a true, physical pain, that she was with Grey. That she had one more chance to explain her pain and her fear of resenting him. That she was safe, tangled in his arms, listening to his steady breaths.

"Get away from me," Mish shrieked while they shouted 'thief' and screamed at her to *get on the ground* and put her *hands up*. Mish ignored them. The terror was so extreme that she could taste it, thick and coppery in her mouth - only it wasn't terror. It was blood from where the guard had struck her with the baton. The pain seeped in, delayed by her surprise but registering in full force now. One of them swung again and this time Mish heard her jaw crack, and her screams were swallowed by the grunting guards and the sounds of hard wood on soft flesh, and soon Mish couldn't hear, or feel, anything at all.

SIXTEEN

Grey was living a nightmare.

Awoken in Mish's bed by the blaring alarms, his first instinct had been to reach for her across the tangle of blankets. She wasn't there. Grey's insides tensed. Instinct told him something terrible was happening. There was no logical reason Mish wouldn't be in bed at this hour, and with that instinct came the inescapable feeling that whatever had happened was his fault, a result of his actions and his lies. He couldn't even think about it, not until he knew Mish was safe. Then he would sort out the whole debacle, lay out his reasoning and pray that her kind nature would extend to forgiveness.

The alarms stopped.

Grey lurched to his feet, spinning the door open and poking his head out into the hallway. His neighbours seemed to have the same idea, a chorus of sleepy faces glancing anxiously at one another and whispering to and fro for information.

A trio of guards rounded the corner, walking in tight formation. Grey understood the severity of the situation by how little they seemed to care for the number of people peeking out after dorm hours and his stomach sank. He knew they were coming for him. Felt it in his bones as surely as he knew those alarms had something to do with Mish.

"Mr. Wright," said one of the masks once they reached him. "Please come with us,"

Grey followed wordlessly, flanked on either side by a guard with the third leading the way. They seemed on edge, their gloved hands fluttering to their batons more often than usual. As if they were waiting for an excuse to use them. The whispers followed them as they walked. He could feel the prickle of curious eyes following him. Grey didn't blame them for speculating. He was speculating himself. He had a million questions and somehow none at all so he held his tongue, content to live in the liminal space where armed escorts could mean anything, and not that Mish had been arrested.

Or sent to the front lines, thought Grey with a violent shudder.

They led him to a clinical white space with a door opposite the one they entered through. Grey's protection detail took their places on either side of it as if he was some sort of threat. The effect was surreal, and Grey felt a moment of disorientation. Was he implicated somehow? What could Mish have gotten herself into that involved him? Had he really been fast asleep a mere twenty minutes ago?

"Wait here," said the third guard, slipping through the doorway.

They returned with a familiar face: his counsellor, looking for all the world like she must sleep in her glasses and perfectly pressed business casual clothes, her purposeless pencil tucked behind her ear. Grey wanted to snatch it away and snap it in two.

"Hello, Grey," she said in the same comforting, clipped tone he remembered. "Please, follow me."

She led him through the door into a small, bright, clean room. It reminded him vaguely of an old operating theatre. Wall-to-ceiling cream-coloured curtains encircled something near the back wall.

"Grey," said the counsellor. He wondered if somebody during her training had told her that overusing somebody's name was comforting. "Something has happened."

"What's behind the curtains?" Grey asked stupidly. Surely there were more important matters to discuss, but he couldn't look away from the curtains hanging like a dark promise.

"I have a few questions for you to answer after which, I will open the curtains. Do you understand?" she surveyed him with unfeeling eyes. Grey stared back, feigning the same indifference.

"Sure."

"What is the nature of your relationship with Mish Taylor?"

Grey's mouth had gone dry, he could hear his tongue prying away from his gums as he spoke. "We are involved," he swallowed. "Cohabitating."

The counsellor nodded, tapping something into her tablet. "Is it true that Ms. Taylor purchased a day pass in your name several weeks ago?"

"It is."

"I see," more tapping. "Have you noticed a recent change in Mish's behaviour?"

Grey hesitated. If Mish was in some sort of trouble the last thing he wanted to do was say something that could incriminate her further. "Not particularly," he said carefully. "She's been a bit quiet."

The counsellor surveyed him critically in a way that reminded Grey of being called to his father's study as a child to be lectured on for some slip up or another. The expression cowed him, just as it had back then, and he found himself staring at the curtains to avoid her eyes.

"Mr. Wright," she said - *apparently we've moved away from informality,* thought Grey - and she adjusted her useless glasses on her ski-slope nose. "I must stress to you that what happened here tonight was completely unprecedented and highly improbable. At MerryCom, we pride ourselves on easing transitions post-reanimation and maintaining the safety of our employees."

"Safety?" asked Grey. A rushing sound in his ears made it difficult to hear and his stomach clenched as if he was falling from a very tall height. Something about the way the counsellor had lingered on the word confirmed something terrible that Grey couldn't bring himself to name. "Where is Mish? What's going on? Is she hurt?"

"There's no easy way to say this,"

Grey hated when people said things like that. What was the point? Certainly not to comfort the receiver. Nothing confirmed terrible news quicker than 'There's no easy way to say this'. Selfish. He wished she would just spit it out.

"There was an attack," said the counsellor finally.

"Mish was attacked?" Grey blurted.

"Well, actually, it appears that she attacked a co-worker and robbed him of his credits," she said.

"That's not possible,"

"She was found attempting to pay her debt at the ticket office,"

"No-,"

"She resisted the guard's attempts to apprehend her," the counsellor ploughed on.

"Stop,"

"There was an altercation between her and the guards. The guards, fearing for their safety responded with appropriate physical measures, and Mish-,"

"I said shut up!" Grey roared. The things she was saying, the lies she was spinning about Mish, *his Mish,* were impossible. She wasn't capable of cruelty, let alone robbery, threatening guards, none of it.

"Mr. Wright, I'm going to ask you to calm down."

"Or what? You'll gas me again?" he spat. "Or will you call your guards in to beat me as well?"

She sat in placid silence while he raged and something in the atmosphere shifted.

"We don't have constructs of religion like you had in your time, but is there a prayer of some kind that you'd like to do?"

Something cold slithered along Grey's spine. Something dark and heavy settled in his chest.

"What's behind the curtain?" he asked, his voice as small as a child's. There was an urge to cry, but it was almost as if his body was acting independently from his emotions. Instead, all of his feelings were locked inside, swirling and frothing like a bottle under pressure. "Please,"

The counsellor uncrossed and recrossed her legs, her discomfort palpable. "I'm sorry for your loss," and she opened the curtain.

Loss.

The word felt foreign in the air, its syllable inappropriately small and delicate considering the magnitude of feeling it contained. Loss was impossible in this context. Grey had lost his keys, his temper more than once; losing people was something else entirely. She must have misspoken. Mish couldn't be *lost.* She wasn't waiting between the couch cushions for him to find.

She was behind the curtain. Arranged on a metal slab behind the cream-coloured folds, hidden beneath a sheet so Grey could only see a shape underneath. But he knew it was her. Knew it the way he knew the curve of her calf and the cut of her collarbones, all of her planes and angles draped in fabric but familiar still. Even as his eyes took her in, his mind rejected the reality.

"What-," he froze mid-sentence, unsure of what he was trying to ask. There were no answers that could satisfy him. "Is…that's not-,"

The counsellor rose to her feet and made her way to the table. She lifted the sheet, gingerly, and tucked it below Mish's neck, as if she were simply sleeping and not lying broken and battered on a gurney.

And broken she was. Her hair, that beautiful mass of inky black curls, was oily slick and matted with blood. Her jaw was crooked at a painful angle and her lips were swollen and split grotesquely. Hollows in her cheeks - missing teeth - and bruises like flower petals on her skin. A gory split where the peak of her collar bone was broken through the skin-

Grey looked away, gagging.

"What did you do to her?" he rounded the room until his gaze fell on the object of his anger. The guard reached for his baton as Grey advanced, his rage swallowing his despair. "*What did you do?*" and he ripped the baton from the guard's hand, smashing it against the opposite wall so hard that it shattered into little splinters. Grey was pleased, let them try to beat the next woman to death with toothpicks.

"*Grey,*" shouted the counsellor as Grey reached for the guard's helmet and he paused.

"Fix her," he said, rounding on the counsellor once more.

"That's not possible," she said, her voice back to irritatingly calm as soon as his hands were back at his sides.

"Bullshit," he spat. "You people can fix anything. *Re-animate her*,"

"You need to understand-,"

"I don't need to understand anything," he said. "Is it money? Whatever it costs, I'll pay it."

"The technology does not exist," said the counsellor. "The damage to her body, it was too much. By the time medics were on the scene there wasn't anything left to save. We can't fix what's completely gone, Grey."

"I don't believe you," he said. "There has to be something," despair crept in along with the urge to touch her. But he held back. Touching her would make it real and it couldn't be real because if it was real it was all his fault. For lying, for not taking her away from this awful place, for choosing his sense of control over her comfort.

"The technology does not exist," said the counsellor.

"Yet," he said. The thought popped into his head, painfully organic, like it had been there all along. "Vitrify her. Store her until it does."

"It's not possible, Mr. Wright, the cost alone-,"

"I told you I would pay it," Grey said, his teeth ground together with his frustration.

"You couldn't possibly-,"

"Call Ashby Salinger. She's my financial advisor at Arcanum," said Grey.

"How do you-," the counsellor stuttered. "I couldn't anyway, not at this hour."

"She'll wake up for me," said Grey, his eyes fixated on Mish's split skin. "For that matter, scan this," he held up his palm.

"Grey-,"

"Do it," Grey's voice was sharp and familiar to him. The same tone he used in the boardroom to establish credibility. The counsellor looked shaken, blinking at the change in Grey's demeanour, but she raised her tablet to his palm all the same.

"How…Grey, how did you-?" she asked shakily.

"Get me Ashby Salinger," he insisted.

*

It turned out that Ashby Salinger was easily motivated to get out of bed once she found out Grey was asking for her. She made it to MerryCom in what seemed to Grey to be under ten minutes, although he wasn't sure how accurate his assessment was. Time had taken on a thick, sticky sort of quality where moments existed in crystallised stillness, and then what could have been hours gushed by in an instant. Still, she arrived all the same, flanked by two guards, looking as perfectly pressed in the middle of the night as she had when he met her.

"Ms. Salinger," said the counsellor by way of greeting. Ashby eyed the counsellor passively in a way that made it clear that she was not impressed with what she saw. Her eyes flickered to Mish's body, which Grey had re-covered with the sheet. Ashby took on a slightly greenish colour, though her expression remained professionally blank.

"Mr. Wright," she placed a gentle hand on his shoulder. The gesture was too intimate to be appropriate, but he appreciated it all the same. "Shall we proceed?"

Grey nodded, numbly, thankful to let somebody else take over for a while. He was lost in a stream of horror and self-hatred that made talking difficult.

"Excellent," she rounded on the counsellor and the guards. "As of 4:02am Mr. Wright had paid his debts and is no longer property of MerryCom. Though you are not privy to my client's financial details, I can assure you that he can afford to freeze Ms. Taylor."

"That's- I mean, I'll have to escalate to management." said the counsellor.

"You do that," said Ashby, completely nonplussed.

The room burst into a billow of conversation as the guards and the counsellor contacted the higher-ups, directing the occasional question to Ashby, who answered smoothly. Grey was a statue beside Mish's body, aware of the activity around him, but only capable of staring down at the sheet.

"Graham Wright?" asked a man's voice. Grey blinked up at him in surprise, unsure of when he had walked in.

"Yes," said Grey, clearing his throat.

"My name is Thomas Serval. I'm the CEO of MerryCom Incorporated," said the man. He looked to be about Grey's age, with an unlined face and salt and pepper hair. Although his dark suit was sophisticatedly well-draped, Grey noted passively that Serval's shirt was misbuttoned.

"Hello, Mr. Serval," said Grey absently. He was long past being impressed by being in the presence of CEOs.

"First, I would like to congratulate you on completing your tenure and welcome you to your second life," said Serval.

"But?" said Grey. He didn't care for niceties. There would be time for all of that once Mish was safely stored away.

Serval rubbed the back of his neck, the gesture straining the seams of his dark suit. "Mr. Wright, Ms. Taylor's body is simply too damaged for our freezing technology to have any effect."

Grey felt rage like a white-hot knife in his back. "I may not know what the laws are at this time, but I promise if you don't start telling me something I want to hear I will sue the ever-loving shit out of this company for wrongful death or whatever your equivalent is. I believe my advisor has informed you of my position, so you know I can afford it."

There was a moment of strained silence while everybody absorbed his words.

Serval cleared his throat uncomfortably. "Look," he said. "I want to help you out here, truly. But the technology simply does not exist at this time, to freeze someone so… altered."

"MerryCom is a massive research and development facility," said Grey calmly. "You're asking me to believe that the leading corporation involved in re-animation has no plans for future advancements?"

Serval sighed. "The closest thing we've had to a breakthrough in the last twenty years is a prototype for superplasma freezing."

"Do that then," said Grey.

"There's no guarantee it would work. All we have is a single prototype that's not even ready to be integrated with the Ark's storage system."

"I don't care. I'll take it," said Grey. "Name your price."

"Mr. Wright, it's-," Serval stammered. "It's a prototype, it's not for sale."

Grey turned his back on Serval and found Ashby leaning casually against the wall. "Can I buy the company?"

Serval spluttered. "Mr. Wright, really-,"

"You can afford to buy the majority of MerryCom's shares, yes." said Ashby, something like awe in her expression.

"Great," said Grey. "Get it done."

"Now really-," said Serval.

"Consider it done," said Ashby, tucking her tablet away with a grin.

"Excellent. Serval, consider this your notice," Grey turned to the counsellor who was watching him with wide eyes. "Prepare the pod for integration to the ark. I want her frozen as soon as possible. And have a team assemble a second pod, with identical technology."

"A second pod?" asked the counsellor.

"For me," said Grey. "I want to wait for her."

"We have many pods suitable for your body that are ready to go now," replied the counsellor.

"No. It has to be the same type. I want us to be reanimated in the same time period, one that has the technology to work with superplasma restoration."

"Can I speak to you?" asked Ashby, drawing him aside by the elbow. "Mr. Wright, I have to warn you, now that you've crystallised your account in our time, it's subject to modern laws. The crypto technology you used last time doesn't exist anymore, not in the same way, anyway. You will not be able to carry your wealth into another reanimation. The law is very clear on that."

"I don't care," said Grey. "I only want her."

SEVENTEEN

A beautiful apartment perched in the treetops lined with windows overlooking the lacy underside of the leaf canopy. Light filtered through the foliage casting the living room in a luminous, golden bath. Far below, the city was an organic snarl of humanity and nature, buildings erupting from the undergrowth like mushroom stalks. The air smelled like honeysuckle and damp earth.

"Hello, handsome," a set of arms wound around his middle and Grey felt the warm press of the body behind him.

A shift in scenery. The familiar blank walls of his dorm at MerryCom. Grey twisted in the embrace and tangled his hands in her hair, marvelling at the inky curls that fell like water through his hands.

"I missed you," he said, bending to kiss her. She tasted the same, cinnamon and toothpaste and home all rolled into one.

"I've only been gone for five minutes," said Mish and her laugh was like sunlight on a stream, and cosy nights under a blanket.

"Too long," said Grey, breathing in the smell of her shampoo and bathing in the incredible relief that she was with him, safe and whole. She pulled away with a smile.

"You could at least make the bed, you know?" she teased, snatching a discarded pillow up off the floor.

There was a hollow pang in Grey's chest growing by the second. The peace wasn't real, couldn't be real after everything that had happened, everything he had done.

"I lied to you," he said before he could think better of it.

"What was that?" Mish didn't look up from fluffing pillows, but Grey watched her. Marvelled at the graceful arc of her neck and the dexterity of her fingers.

"I lied about the money," he said. "I had it all along. I hid it because I was scared."

Mish turned to him and frowned. "Who says you get to make all of the rules?" she raised one eyebrow and crossed her arms.

"Mish, I'm telling you that I lied to you," said Grey. "I took your day pass, and I recovered the account and I lied to you about it."

Mish grinned, winding her arms around his neck, "Maybe I want to stay in bed and eat ice cream all day."

"Would you listen to me?" snapped Grey. Mish froze, her playful expression unmoving as the dorm walls flickered like a broken laptop screen.

Back in the treetop apartment Grey cursed, reaching for a small box on a side table. He fumbled it open with shaking hands, retrieving the cube shaped object inside. He pressed it to his lips, inhaling deeply. The sedative slipped into his lungs with a delicious wave of comfort.

Back in the dorm, Mish's fingers teased the strip of skin below his shirt, drawing goosebumps across his hip bones with familiar little circles.

"And maybe," she said, leaning forward to place a little nipping kiss on his neck, "I want a dog."

Grey groaned at the sensation of her warm breath on his throat, his hand coming to her hips as she kissed her way up his neck, across his jaw, before finally capturing his mouth. His response was immediate. He lifted her off the floor and pressed her against the wall. She responded by wrapping her legs around his waist and running her fingers through his hair, angling his head exactly where she wanted him. It was less like kissing and more like consuming. Grey panted into her sighs as clothing was ripped away and suddenly there was nothing between them but air.

Grey paused, taking a moment to marvel at her. Mish squirmed in his arms, pulling him closer.

"Just wait a minute," said Grey, his throat thick with emotion. The fire in Mish's eyes dimmed slightly as she shifted. She released her legs and stood under her own steam, peeking up at him seductively from below her thick lashes.

"Where do you want me?" she asked, her voice soft. Grey blinked at her, uneasiness washing over him. The features were Mish, but the submissive posture was off somehow.

"I just-," Grey paused, unsure of what to say.

Mish's face twisted into a wicked smile. "Do you want to watch?" her hand trailed tauntingly over her collarbone, across her breast, lower still, her eyes growing heavy-lidded as her skin flushed. She was magnificent, absolutely gorgeous, aroused and palpably alive in the dim lighting and Grey ached to touch her. But when he reached for her she froze for a beat, always a half-step behind with her responses. The walls flickered once more.

"Fuck it," Grey growled, ending the simulation. The remote didn't shatter when he hurled it against the wall, but it made a satisfying *bang!*

He glanced around the open expanse of his apartment, taking in the high ceilings and polished floors and immaculate cream furniture as his breath settled. He even took an extra hit of his sedative, but the ache in his chest didn't fade.

It had been the same for weeks. He would begin to forget, let himself start to enjoy his new life as one of the wealthiest men in the world, only to have the fantasy come crashing down around him. Mish was dead, her body frozen in a pod locked deep below the ground, while a sister pod was being constructed to slot in beside hers, and Grey was alone.

And it was all his fault.

If he had only told her about the money. If she had only told him how bad things had really got. But even that was his fault. Of course, in all her goodness, Mish wouldn't want him to feel guilty for "wasting her credits".

Not wasted. Stolen, Grey thought nastily. He always ended up back there, questioning his own arrogance. *You thought you could make choices for her, that you knew better than her, that you knew what she needed, and you got her killed for it.*

The irony of him living the life Mish had died dreaming of seemed exceptionally cruel. His great big kitchen mocked him with its unused appliances, his bed sat empty. Sisyphus, finally at the mountain's peak only to find a second, far worse curse.

Hollow.

Grey lurched to his feet. Ashby was right. He was spending too much time alone cooped up in the apartment. His self-flagellation wasn't going to speed up the building process. He could spend every waking moment with Mish simulations, but he would only notice the seams more and more. There wasn't a computer program on earth that could capture all of the bits and pieces that made up Mish. It was time to get out and meet his fellow man, to take advantage of the society that Mish was so desperate to be part of.

His transition manager, Leaf, was always pushing him to take a tour of the city. Provided by Arcanum to ease Grey's transition from menial worker to economically influential shareholder. Leaf was a young, but obviously successful man. Born and raised Proto, Grey might have found it hard to like him, but Leaf was a cheery sort with whom Grey might have had a beer or two with in another lifetime. He approached Grey's growing agoraphobia with gentle determination, calling weekly to offer classes or hobbies or mixers. Anything that would draw Grey away from his misery. *Nobody knows who you are out here,* Leaf would reassure him. *You're rich enough to keep your riches secret. Do classical dance, do cookery classes, do whatever you want, no worries at all.*

Leaf was thrilled when Grey called asking to book the tour. "That's very gree, Grey, good on you." Oftentimes Leaf's youth shone through his indecipherable slang.

"Thank you?"

"It's *great, really.* I'm glad you're getting out," Leaf said with a laugh. "I'll have a transport waiting outside in five."

Grey thanked him and paced around his apartment, suddenly ablaze with nervous energy. *It's no big deal,* he told himself. *Just a tour. I can knock out that med scan Ashby has been bothering me about.* That was better. It was easier to leave his treetop nest when he had a real purpose.

Grey slid into the transport with Leaf, grateful to find that it would be a private tour. He suspected Leaf was easing him into re-joining society and was being careful not to push too much social interaction on him at once. Grey reminded himself to contact Ashby about giving Leaf a raise.

"Entering: Financial District," said the disembodied voice of the transport. Here the buildings grew taller and with bigger and brighter windows. The transport smoothly informed him that most workers split their time between working from home and in the office. Wages were tied to productivity with corporations operating under a profit cap and workers splitting whatever remained. There were no work weeks, no clocking in and out, no 9-5 commutes at all. Workers were assigned tasks which, once completed, meant that their time was their own. With the company's success directly affecting the worker's income, it was in everyone's best interest to do their work and do it well. And of course, those who didn't wish to work could find a basic income model fitting for their needs and were enabled to pursue further education or the arts. Though far from what Grey had imagined from watching Star Trek growing up, it was a clever system. Lucky for him, he supposed, since it meant his wealth still had value.

"You ever heard of the fake jobs theory?" said Grey. Leaf peeled his gaze from the view and turned to face Grey.

"Nyup,"

Grey assumed this meant no. "Well, back in the 21st century we had enormous loops of 'non-jobs'."

"Why would people do jobs that had no point?" Said Leaf.

"It wasn't by conscious design," said Grey, leaning towards the window to assess the glassy, jaggedly shaped splinter-like finance buildings. "But across most big companies, huge swathes of people's jobs involved creating work, which got passed to someone else to action and modify. Then that person would pass it on, and so on and so forward until the work reached the original creator again. Then the cycle would start again." Grey could see Leaf looked a little blank, so he continued, "For instance, most of somebody's job could involve being sent a PowerPoint slide deck, breaking it apart, and piecing it back together again before sending it on, never really seeing any end impact of their work. Tragic and deluded, really."

Leaf smiled and nodded, as if he politely accepted that he'd never really understand what Grey was saying.

Grey saw a large neon sign saying Confession Booths in the back of the financial district, which confused Grey as he had established that there was no more religion. Leaf explained that it was mostly for theatre and therapy, you didn't need to confess things you'd actually done, it was just a confidential pay-to-play experience, for fun really. Grey contemplated a visit.

After the financial district came the arts district. Grey liked it better there, where amphitheatres and galleries dotted the streets along with elaborate stonework sculptures. There were paintings with colours more vivid that Grey had ever imagined and the echoes of musicians ringing throughout. It was a place of perfect beauty and Grey felt a pang, knowing that Mish would have loved it.

For all the impressive works surrounding him, Grey's favourite were the sculpted trees. Trees tall as skyscrapers pruned and twisted and encouraged to grow into beautiful shapes. There was a woman, bathing by the river, her body reclined and consisted of a twisted witch elm and her hair a streak of leaves. Her roots, which were also her feet, trailing into the river below. She was a perfect likeness and a perfect tree, so when Grey looked at her, he could see both tree and woman simultaneously and separately. It was the most incredible optical illusion Grey had ever seen. And there were more! Just past the tree woman was another sculpted tree, or perhaps several trees, this time coaxed into a mountain. A volcano, in fact, judging by the way the leaves resembled a great cloud of ash stretching above.

Turning to Leaf, Grey tried again to share a musing from his time.

"Sick Building Syndrome," he said. "That's another thing you probably don't have now." Leaf, ever dutiful, waited for Grey to explain.

"Once, I worked on a deal to modernise a housing block called Metro Central Heights. It was in Elephant and Castle in south—well, it doesn't matter. Anyway, months after it opened, people who lived there started to suffer from symptoms of chronic illness— headaches, trouble concentrating, breathing problems, all kinds of things. Heaps of investigations found no cause, and instead led to a diagnosis of Sick Building Syndrome - an inexplicable combination of architectural and design features that make people ill. A repaint, a new entrance and a gym seemed to fix it."

Leaf again nodded his affirmation that he had listened. Grey regretted leaving the arts district when the transport slid away and continued its slow-paced amble through the city. They stopped at a crossroad where one road pointed towards the mountain and MerryCom beyond while the other stretched to the right, past the treeline and into oblivion.

"Wait," said Grey as the transport turned towards the mountain. "Where does the other one lead?"

"To the Outer Tenements," said the transport. "Outside of the city,"

"I want to see it," said Grey.

"Not recommended," said the transport. "Safety compromised due to civil unrest,"

"I don't care," said Grey, a creeping familiarity coming over him. "Take me there,"

The transport stilled for a moment, then rotated to the right. The light dimmed as they approached the tree line at the edge of the city. The sunlight seemed to stay trapped eerily in the trees and obscure the darkness beyond. Grey rubbed his shoulder absently, feeling the memory of the bullet. The scar was long gone, but the old man's screams had never left him.

Leaf excused himself to the back of the transport to take a call.

"Now entering: Outer Tenements," said the transport as they slid past the last row of trees and into darkness.

Grey's first impression was that they had driven into the ruins of a huge city. The dotted asphalt and concrete buildings that stretched along an acidic-looking river felt familiar, clearly leftover from his proto life or soon after. Nature had done its best to reclaim the space, but rather than the lush garden-covered balconies and roofs in the city, only scraggly weeds scraped their way out of the cracks and potholes here. Overhead, the clouds hung heavy and sickly green, so suffocatingly close the Grey thought he might be able to step out of the transport and touch them.

As Grey watched, a shadow pried itself from the crumbling remains of an office building and crept among the rocks and debris alongside the transport. It was a man, a tall spider-thin man with shreds of clothing on him as black as the asphalt under his feet. He moved languidly, keeping pace with the transport with a strange catlike grace. The man darted from low stone cover to cover. Grey found himself staring at the man's face, trying to capture his features in his mind. The hollow cheeks, the bruises shadowed deep under one missing eye, the longing and distrust in his expression.

There was a familiar rumble across the river and the hair on the back of Grey's neck rose. Flashes of light lit up the horizon and smoke billowed and spiralled to join the heaving clouds above. Grey realised the man must have run from this battle zone. He felt a camaraderie with the man, as he had come from that dark place as well and he leaned forward, wishing the man could see him through the opacity of the transport vehicle. He wanted the man to recognise him somehow.

The transport slid through the city ruins and into a mud-slung shanty town. The man stopped at the edge, eyeing the transport as it slid past. Grey could see hints of movement here and there - the flutter of a tent flap, the smoking remnants of a fire, a slim hand dragging a bucket behind a shed - the only indication that people lived there at all.

"Why is this here?" asked Grey. "Who are these people?"

"The Outer Tenements are comprised of individuals who chose not to participate in our society," said the transport.

"Right. They 'chose'," said Grey with a scoff. He thought about the rows and rows of unawakened 21st century bodies in their pods, delayed for re-vitrification because there was no space for them in this world. "Did they choose to go to war too?"

The transport didn't respond to that, just scuttled back towards the city, through the tree line, returning them to the idyllic sun-dappled greenery once more. Grey's gaze was fixed on the darkness he'd just left behind, his shoulder aching, unable to focus on the beauty ahead.

"What are they fighting for?" he asked finally, his shoulder aching. The transport didn't respond - not that he'd really expected it to.

*

"Have you noticed any mood changes?" asked Healer Sullivan when Grey emerged from the MedScan tube. It was an incredible piece of technology, Grey thought. A man-sized tube, similar to the shower facilities he had used at MerryCom, only this he climbed into fully clothed. Once sealed, the tube emitted a soft humming sound that the healers had explained as a sort of radiation free MRI scan that would detect and diagnose all sorts of medical issues.

"Not really," said Grey. He shook his head, his ears feeling waterlogged for a moment.

Healer Sullivan smiled placidly. They had warned Grey that he might feel a little strange after his first scan. Reanimated bodies were a little more delicate than the Protos of this time.

"What about dips in energy? Any aches and pains?" asked Healer Sullivan.

Grey shrugged. Any changes in his mood or physicality could obviously be credited to losing Mish. He blinked suspiciously at the MedScan tube. Could it diagnose depression? Did they even have depression in this century? It seemed like an ancient sort of illness.

"Well, Mr. Wright," said the healer, tucking away his tablet and regarding Grey calmly. "You have the beginnings of a benign tumour just below your pituitary gland,"

"I- what?" asked Grey. He shook his head again, clearing the non-existent water from his ears. "That's in my brain, right? It's a brain tumour."

"Yes."

Grey thought Healer Sullivan looked frustratingly calm considering the gravity of the news.

"Well, um, benign, yeah?" He swallowed, his mouth uncomfortably dry. "That's not cancer at least. That's good, right?"

"This type of craniopharyngioma is rarely cancerous, yes, but it does present some danger," said the healer. "Damage to the hormone regulation centre in the pituitary gland, pressure to the brain tissues as it grows, personality changes, it's definitely a problem. In fact, according to your scan, this tumour will kill you in approximately twelve years."

Grey gaped at the doctor, so confused by his calm demeanour that he was completely speechless for a moment. He sank into a heavily cushioned chair across the room and stared at the wall, bewildered.

"Mr. Wright? Are you okay?" asked Healer Sullivan.

"You just told me I'm going to die in twelve years. How could I be okay?" asked Grey.

Healer Sullivan blinked, confused. Then, he jolted to his feet so suddenly that Grey startled.

"Oh, heavens, I completely forgot," he exclaimed, a sheepish smile creeping across his features. "Tumours were often fatal in your time, but we treat them with a simple in-office procedure. You're in absolutely no danger. I'm so sorry to have frightened you."

Grey eyed the healer's creeping smile and thought for a moment that he wasn't sorry at all. In fact, he seemed to be treating the misunderstanding like some sort of prank. Grey wondered if he, like the people in the street who hissed at him once they recognised him as a Rainy, found some sort of personal pleasure in mocking him. Could the prejudice reach as far as healthcare professionals?

He shook his head. He wasn't going to push it. The sneers and jabs were quickly becoming a common part of life. When he did bother to venture out, he was met with suspicion and oftentimes outright aggression. His money could only shield him so well from the Protos' disdain. The money seemed to make it worse for some of them. To be lifted so high with money earned from a dying planet didn't sit well with some people. There was no point in fighting a hatred that ran that deep.

"So," Grey said, his voice hoarse. "An in-office procedure? Is it some kind of surgery?"

"Of course not," said Healer Sullivan, as if he could imagine nothing more barbaric than surgery. "If you'll kindly step back into the tube…"

*

Grey mused on the fact that had he not died, he would have likely died anyway a decade later. Perhaps that was one less regret to worry about. That night Grey celebrated defeating his brain tumour with another trip to the simulation chamber. This time he logged in a different memory; one he hadn't thought about in a long time. Not since those long nights back at MerryCom, lying in bed tossing, turning, and replaying the day's interactions with Mish like a child with his first crush.

"Terrible technique," said Mish with a devious little grin.

"Concentric circles," said Grey, demonstrating with the wet mop on the floor. "It's the ultimate move. Look at that floor, you could eat off of it,"

"Absolutely not. Figure eight or bust," said Mish. "Clean and efficient," and the sunlight filtering through the windows of the breezeway seemed to tangle in her curls, splashing the tips with fire. Her mouth was happy and relaxed, full lips split into the mischievous smile he loved, that he had missed for so long.

"Fine. We'll race," he said.

And they were off, starting on either end of the breezeway and mopping with all of the competitive intensity of Olympians. Only Mish was right - *wasn't she always?* - and when it became clear that she was going to reach the middle first, Grey threw down his mop and wrapped his arms around her middle, spinning her away from her mop while she kicked and shriek-laughed. He dropped her back on her side of the breezeway and raced back to his mop, slipping in the sudsy puddles to her absolute delight.

She swung her mop wide, pelting him with soapy water while he roared with laughter and returned the favour, the situation dissolving into an all-out water fight, the mopping forgotten entirely.

"I surrender, I surrender!" gasped Mish between giggles. Grey had given up on the water and moved on to tickling. It was game cover once he realised that she had an especially sensitive spot just below her ribs.

And Grey rewound the simulation from there. From that perfect moment. Mish frozen in the setting sun, surrounded by their water mess, head thrown back with delight, and eyes streaming with laughter, back to his sloppy concentric circles and a contest he would never win, even though he was pretty sure he already had.

EIGHTEEN

"Thank you for meeting with me, Mr. Wright," said the newly reinstated Thomas Serval. It turned out that shareholders, even those in the majority, couldn't decide to fire a CEO unilaterally. Not that Grey minded. His frustration with Serval faded as soon as Mish was safely settled in the Ark's storage pod.

Grey wandered into the office, expansive and covered in the MerryCom signature antiseptic white, with a wall of crystal-clear glass that overlooked the valley below. It was the sort of view Grey would have been infinitely impressed with in his former life. An intimidation tactic and a status symbol all in one. He thought about that life distantly now, staring at the lush greenery below with a disinterest that surprised him. When had his priorities shifted so drastically? It was as if Mish had reached into his chest and pulled out the pieces of him that coveted material things. He wondered what she had left him with.

"Of course, Mr. Serval," said Grey as he lowered himself into a plush, white chair opposite Serval's desk. He arranged his features into something that he hoped resembled polite interest rather than his detachment.

"I assumed you would be ready for an update on the prototype," said Serval, lowering himself into the chair behind the desk.

That pricked Grey's interest. His pulse jumped to his throat at the mention, but he kept his features still. It was as if Mish's death had rubbed his skin raw somehow, created a new fragility in his flesh, and if he let himself hope he was certain he'd shatter. He kept his voice even.

"I am,"

"It's coming along nicely based on the original prototype. I suspect it will be finished any day now," said Serval delicately. "Though, the process is taking longer now that the original is occupied."

"Understandable," said Grey. Underneath the fog of his grief, Grey wanted to reassure Serval that he wasn't a complete arsehole. That the emotionally ravaged wildness had left him since their last meeting, and they were on an even footing.

"I must say, I find it curious that you haven't paid for any of your fellow Rainy friends to be released," muttered Serval cautiously.

Grey stayed silent. He couldn't bring himself to see any of them after what happened. They were all Mark's friends, and it stung him to think about Mark at all.

Serval sat back in his chair.

"Mr. Wright, I know your financial advisor has gone over this process with you. The material facts of re-vitrification-,"

"That it might not work, yes," said Grey. "That I will lose my fortune, yes."

Serval's eyes narrowed briefly, as close to a wince as he could come without being inappropriate. "Good. Good. That's… that's excellent, yes."

Grey considered the man for a moment. "But you have concerns?"

"I'm afraid I do," said Serval, his shoulders lifting to his ears as if he was bracing for impact. "As a, er, business partner of sorts, I worry about the impact on the company when our majority shareholder re-vitrifies."

"I appreciate that," said Grey, his eyes drifting to the wall of windows behind Serval's back. A hawk circled the valley in lazy sweeping loops. Grey was gripped with a sudden longing for a bird's eye view.

"But?" prompted Serval.

Grey sighed and adjusted his posture in the chair. "To be frank, I don't care about the company, or anything in this world."

Serval's lips were a tight white line. "I see," he said tightly. "And your shares?"

"As I said, I really don't care. Even if I could take them with me, I don't think I would want to," said Grey.

He could tell his answer disappointed Serval by the way his brow furrowed, and he understood why. Serval was still operating in a world of money and success. Really, if they had existed in the same proto-life Grey imagined he and Serval would have been colleagues, maybe almost-friends. The ambitious and entrepreneurial man that Grey was back then, and probably still would be if not for Mish, hadn't realised that it was people who made life beautiful.

"Well, Mr. Wright," said Serval, pulling Grey from his thoughts. "You have a couple of options. You have no next of kin, so we can sell your shares and donate the funds. There are a range of causes you can consider gifting them."

"Why don't I let you and Ashby handle all of that?" Grey said flippantly.

Serval's shoulders relaxed. "Of course, I would be happy to, Mr. Wright. Very happy to."

"That's settled then," said Grey, his eyes returning to the hawk. They sat in silence for a moment and Grey could feel Serval considering his next words.

"That settles the business end," said Serval. "But can I talk to you as a fellow human being?"

Grey tore his eyes from the window and met Serval's gaze. "Sure."

"We can re-vitrify you," he said. "We can store your body, store Mish's body, practically indefinitely. But the technology to bring you back… there's no guarantee it will ever exist. The reanimation program is failing, Mr. Wright. The public simply doesn't support it."

"Yes, they've made that abundantly clear," said Grey.

"There is an admitted prejudice against Rainies, it's true."

Grey only smiled, gesturing for Serval to go on.

"Without public support, there's no guarantee that the program will be funded in the future. Without funding there is no re-animation," said Serval.

"I see," said Grey, blithely. Serval considered him for a long moment while Grey held his gaze comfortably.

"I can see that I won't change your mind."

"That is correct."

Serval slunk out from behind his desk, sparing a passing glance to the impressive view. He moved on so quickly that Grey was certain he hadn't noticed the hawk at all. Serval leaned back against his desk and scratched his chin.

"You're a braver man than I am," he said after a while. "She must have really been something."

"She really is." said Grey.

*

Grey found himself wandering the familiar halls of MerryCom. It was nearing the end of the workday, when most Protos would be tucked inside their various offices and the Rainies were relegated to cleaning the lower levels. In his time here, Grey had assumed the separation was devised to maintain an air of professionalism between the classes, but now he realised it was to keep the Rainies motivated. The entire program was based around the Rainies' desperation to pay their debt and join society. Grey thought Rainy work ethic might slip if they knew they were working to join a society that had very little use for them. It was comforting, wandering the empty white halls with no Protos sneering at him for re-animating. The ones that didn't hate him for being a Rainy hated him for cheating the system and rising to an exorbitant wealth he was beginning to realise he had never really deserved.

He crossed the breezeway, feeling the mist off of the waterfall curling around him, taking in a lungful of sweet-smelling air. Something was shifting inside of him, the familiar weight that had settled on his chest shuffling slightly so that he could feel an echo of himself beneath the grief. That old ambition still burned somewhere deep inside him, but changed, the way everything had changed after Mish.

He wondered, for the first time, what he would do if he were planning to stay. If re-vitrification wasn't an option. If he were to truly integrate into society. It had seemed like such an impossibility on that day, long ago, when he was staring up at the Arcanum building with spittle on his shirt, but now he had money. More money and more power than anybody could ever hope to wield in a lifetime. He could change anything if he only had the mind to.

"Is that you, Grey?" a soft voice pulled him from his thoughts. It was Cherry, her curtain of thick blonde hair tied at the nape of her neck, mop in hand.

"Guilty," said Grey, breaking into an easy grin that surprised him. "How are you, Cherry?"

She smiled back, a gentle, almost sad gesture. "I'm sticking it out," she said. Grey frowned, noting the circles under her eyes, the tired way she clutched at the mop.

"It's good to see you," he said, unwilling to press her.

"You too," she said. "Look at you. You really made it out, huh?"

Grey blinked. "I did, yeah."

"That's great. There were rumours - compensation for what happened, but they don't tell us much down here," said Cherry. "But I don't have to tell you that. Mark said... well, Mark doesn't really say much of anything anymore. Not since Mish."

Grey felt his fingernails dig into his palm. There was a rage in him, deep-seeded and raw and probably unjustified, but in him all the same.

"I'm so sorry," Cherry went on, either oblivious to his discomfort or kind enough not to acknowledge it. "You really do look great, Grey. Freedom agrees with you."

Grey cleared his throat and looked away toward the waterfall until the lump in his throat dissolved enough for him to talk. "Listen, Cherry," he said. "Maybe you can help me with something."

"Of course," she said gently.

"I've been thinking. I want to understand what attracted all of us to vitrification in the first place," he said. "It's very personal, I know, but I want to find a way to help us all integrate better and think this might be an important part of that."

Cherry considered him for so long that Grey was certain she was about to walk away. Her brow furrowed, and her lips parted a little. Grey felt a wash of embarrassment, worried he had crossed a line. He had always liked Cherry, the last thing he wanted to do was make her uncomfortable.

"I'll tell you," she said finally. "But you have to do something for me first."

"What's that?" asked Grey, surprised.

Cherry's lips curled in a gesture that might have been a smile if it weren't for the sadness in her eyes. "Won't you talk to him?" she said. She must have noticed Grey stiffen because her knuckles tightened on the mop. "He hasn't been right since- since what happened."

Grey turned away, staring at the setting sun until his breath steadied.

"It wasn't his fault," said Cherry, her voice so soft it could have been the wind. "The guards- it's like they were waiting for one of us to step out of line. They jumped at the chance to hurt her. And Mark... he doesn't sleep, he's not eating. I can't watch him hurt anymore, Grey."

"Fine," said Grey before he could talk himself out of it. "Lead the way."

She nodded with another unreadable smile, led him across the breezeway, and then paused. The setting sun backlit her, curling the tips of her hair into a modest halo of light as she considered him.

"I didn't want to miss out," she said. "I was always so afraid of being left behind, left alone. So, I made sure I couldn't be. Does that make any sense?"

Grey smiled back at her, squinting into the sunlight. "Absolutely."

NINETEEN

The first thing Grey noticed were the dark circles under Mark's eyes, like purple and yellow flower petals pressed into the delicate skin. Cherry was right. He had lost weight. Grey could see the outline of his collarbones through his uniform shirt. His eyes looked sunken and haunted, his hair tousled and dirty, his mouth in a tight line devoid of his usual cheery grin. The effect was unsettling.

Grey cleared his throat and formed a strangled "Hi."

If possible, Mark's lips thinned even more, and when he spoke his voice sounded thick and rusty from disuse. "Hey."

Mark's eyes darted from Grey to Cherry, who was standing behind him, still clutching the mop with nervous hands. Mark simply stood in his doorway, not inviting them in.

"I thought you should talk," she said in her calm, even voice.

Mark's gaze found Grey again, his expression unreadable. Grey felt a pang of frustration. What right did Mark have to be walking around looking so bloody *broken?* After all, if he hadn't called the guards…

"I'll leave you two to work things out," said Cherry, breaking the silence. She nodded encouragingly at both of them before turning and making her way down the hall. And then it was just Grey and Mark. Alone at last.

"So," said Mark after another minute of tense silence. "Are you here to hit me, or-?"

"Of course not," said Grey, although his fists were clenched at his sides. He made a conscious effort to relax them.

"You can if you want," said Mark. "We both know I deserve it," he pushed away from the doorway and threw himself into his desk chair, gesturing to Grey to come inside. Grey did, wincing as the door slid shut behind him. He wasn't sure if he should sit or not, but it felt strange towering over Mark. He settled for leaning against the wall.

"I don't know what to say to that," Grey said, surprised at his own honesty.

Mark pinched the bridge of his nose and exhaled very tiredly.

"When was the last time you slept?" asked Grey. "You look like hell."

"I feel like it," said Mark. "I don't sleep much lately. When I do manage to fall asleep, I have these dreams…," he trailed off, his eyelids sliding closed.

Grey found himself nodding. "You and me both."

Mark's shoulders slumped at his words. "I just keep replaying it over and over again in my head. What I should have said - how I could have stopped her."

Grey pried his hands open finger by finger, relishing the aching release of tension. He flexed each digit, staring at the ground, unable to meet Mark's eyes. It had taken him a long time to accept Mish's part in all of it. He still couldn't quite picture her in this dorm, so desperate for escape that she would hold a piece of glass to Mark's throat. He knew his friend wanted forgiveness, needed it the way a dying man needed water, but Grey couldn't bring himself to do it.

"If I could go back I would do it all differently. I would never call the guards. God, Grey, I never would have if I knew they were capable-,"

"But you did know, didn't you?" said Grey, his voice dark and rough now. "You knew how the Protos feel about us. Because you've been out there, Mark. You saw all of that hate and it kept you here at MerryCom."

Mark paled, half surprised that Grey knew, his lips a near bluish-white and his eyes wide. "I didn't," he said. "I really didn't. Out there, sure. But not here. Not at MerryCom. Six years here for me, and the guards never went beyond a shove, a threat, a slap on the wrist. This was supposed to be a safe place. That's why I stayed. I'm pretty sure that's why you stayed too."

It was Grey's turn to pale. "I don't know what you're talking about."

"I think you and I need to be honest with each other," said Mark. "For Mish."

Grey stared at the floor. He couldn't look at Mark. He didn't trust himself not to leap across the room and throttle him. And he couldn't bear to see his own humiliation and guilt mirrored in Mark's expression.

"For Mish," Grey agreed. "We both let her down," the admission felt like falling from a very high height, the way his stomach swooped and clenched. "I was going to get us both out. I just needed time to come up with a plan. I didn't know how to keep what we had safe."

Mark nodded, his throat bobbing as he swallowed. "Nobody understands until they've seen what it's like out there. How overwhelming it can be."

"Least of all, her," said Grey. "She was so idealistic, you know? Always assuming the best of people… I underestimated her."

Mark ran a shaking hand through his dirty hair. "I thought she was sick," he said. "She came to my room that night and I told her everything. I tried to warn her about what was waiting out there, but she wasn't having any of it. I didn't put together what happened until after I heard you got your freedom. I just thought she was having an episode or something. I assumed they'd hold her for a psych eval or sedate her, not… not what they did. It wasn't until Cherry told me about the day pass that I put it all together. You always had the money, didn't you?"

"Yes," said Grey. "Yes, I did. I guess you and I are the same after all."

"What chance did Mish have with friends like us?" said Mark bitterly. Grey sighed. The anger had drained out of him, leaving him shaky and sweating but also lighter somehow.

Grey plodded over to the bed and sat on the corner, elbows resting on his knees and his head in his hands. He took a deep breath, exhaling shakily.

"Why did you vitrify?" he asked.

Mark let out a barking sound that Grey realised was a laugh, pained and raw. "I was an arrogant bastard, Grey. I thought I had accomplished everything a person could do in that lifetime, so I went off looking for another."

Grey nodded softly to himself. "We really are similar."

Mark's mouth turned up in a close approximation of a smile. "Why are you asking?"

Grey chewed on the inside of his cheek for a moment, searching for a name to put to the idea that had been building inside of him ever since his meeting that afternoon. Longer even, maybe when he had taken the tour out to the slums.

"I'm going to start a programme. Maybe an evening school, after shift ends," he said. "I want to teach the other Rainies about the outside world. Educate them. Maybe start a programme to train them for modern jobs."

Mark's eyebrows lifted practically to his hairline. "That's brilliant, Grey. Really."

"It's wrong, the way they keep us in the dark here," said Grey. "MerryCom has profited off of Rainy ignorance for too long. We can't be the only ones who were frightened into staying."

Mark nodded along with him, his eyes brightening slightly. Not quite his usual mischievous glint, but a vast improvement from his hollow-eyed stare.

"I love it," he said.

"Will you help?" asked Grey.

Mark's face fell into serious lines once again. "Are you sure?"

Grey took a deep breath through his nose and let it out, running his tongue against the ragged ridge on the inside of his cheek.

"I am," he said. "Maybe we can both find a little redemption."

*

Finding a historian turned out to be easier than Grey anticipated. If there was anything the Protos valued more than their environmentally sustainable cities, it was remembering past mistakes. It took longer for Grey to track down a library with all of the unreadable signs that it did to find

Professor Amy Brent, who as it happened, had taught Xander many years before.

Amy was an academic historian with a focus on pre-war environmental politics. She was a harsh-mannered woman in her sixties, slow to smile but entirely unfazed by Grey's Rainy mannerisms and strange requests. She took to teaching Rainies with incredible fervour, and while she would never be considered 'inviting', she was deeply invested in her students' success.

The class was a near-instant hit. Mark hit the ground running as soon as Grey had secured Amy and bullied MerryCom into letting them use the empty canteen in the evenings. He spread the word to the other Rainies, spoke with the other supervisors to arrange schedules for the ones who worked nights, and infected the rest of them with his enthusiasm for the project. It was startling for Grey walking into the canteen on that first night of class to see Amy scowling and lecturing to a canteen that was absolutely packed with filled seats. She pulled up her presentation, a syllabus for surviving and thriving in the outside world: from history, to philosophy, to everyday skills like navigating public transport.

The only ones who seemed to be against the project were Grey's colleagues at MerryCom. He had been right in assuming that the company's policies regarding educating Rainies had very little to do with a lack of resources and everything to do with keeping them purposefully ignorant of the world outside the compound.

"It's not good for them," Serval had said when Grey approached the board with his plan. "Better to shield them from the truth as long as we can."

But Grey saw through it. Serval may have convinced himself that he was protecting the Rainies, but all he was really doing was protecting the company's bottom line. It was harder to lead people with choices down the path you decided on for them.

In the end, Serval's opinion hadn't mattered. As the overwhelming majority shareholder, Grey had the final say on the majority of MerryCom's policies. He had had to pause the plans to transfer his shares into a trust for Ashby and Serval to manage after his re-vitrification, which created a bit of rift between him and the CEO, but as he watched the Rainies re-discover the world around them he found it increasingly difficult to care about Serval's agenda.

It was something Mish had understood long before Grey, but then, she had always seen much more clearly than he did. Grey spent his evenings among the Rainies, sitting in on Amy's lectures and learning along with them, and slowly things began to change. Suddenly his world was full of community and laughter. The hazy fog lifted around him and he could taste food again, could feel things to his core again and he realised that it was the people around him breathing life into him, sharpening each moment into something special.

He continued asking questions, still desperate to understand the motivation behind the one overwhelming thing that bound the Rainies: why vitrification? The answers turned out to be much the same across the board. The process was always expensive, so most were financially successful like him or gifted their vitrification from some wealthy benefactor like Mish. But it was more than the economic classes that made them similar. There was an overall longing in them, a fixation on the future and planning the steps to get there. A consumerist's need to squeeze every bit of affluence life could give them. It was a feeling Grey was particularly familiar with.

"So, what changed it for you?" asked Mark after Grey explained his findings. They had resumed their long walks in the evenings after class ended for the day. Working on the programme together had thawed their friendship, though Grey doubted they would ever reach their former easy comfort.

"Mish, of course, and I guess, all of you. It wasn't just one thing," Grey smiled down at his shoes, rubbing the back of his neck with one hand. "You know, I had this girlfriend back in the day."

"Oh yeah?"

"Mmmhmm," said Grey. "Sally. She tried to tell me. She warned me that I was going down the wrong path. Called my life *hollow*."

Mark winced. "Ouch. Sounds like a nice lady."

Grey laughed. "She was wonderful. Much smarter than me. Smarter than I was capable of giving her credit for."

"Well, it doesn't take much to be smarter than you," said Mark, but his smile was gentle. "Did she knock some sense into you after all of this time?"

"I think she did," said Grey, feeling a gentle ache in his chest. He wondered what the rest of her life became. He hoped she'd married. Hoped she had lots of babies to pass on that razor-sharp wisdom onto. Hoped she spent lovely autumn-strewn days drinking wine and having picnics.

"I think education is making you soft," said Mark, gently pulling Grey from his thoughts.

"Yeah, yeah," laughed Grey. "I doubt it'll last. We've got the job training programme to get off the ground."

"Serval is still giving you trouble?"

"Always," said Grey. "He doesn't see the value in allocating more company resources to another training programme."

Mark frowned. "Another Rainy programme, you mean."

Grey's smile was wry. "Unfortunately for him, I *am* the company's resources."

Mark barked out a laugh. "I always knew we'd beat some humour into you. You've still got a bit of an ego though."

Grey laughed with Mark, shoving his shoulder like they were mischievous children and not grown men discussing improving the future of their people. It was a melancholy sort of happiness, made all the sweeter for the shadows.

"You're chiming," said Mark after a moment, gesturing to Grey's pocket.

He was right and Grey pulled out his tablet, steeling himself for another contentious conversation with Serval.

Only, it wasn't Serval.

"What's wrong?" asked Mark. "You've gone all white."

"They've finished the pod," said Grey through dry lips. "They're ready whenever I am."

"Oh, wow, that's-," Mark swallowed. "I mean, what are you going to do?"

Grey tucked the tablet back into his pocket and didn't answer. For the first time, he wasn't sure how to take the next step.

TWENTY

Grey hesitated before re-entering the simulation chamber he'd had built into his apartment. He liked to save the chamber for moments of particular difficulty, preferring to use the portable headset in his living room. He used the stationary chamber on those nights when his missing Mish felt like a physical wound in his chest and nothing but full immersion would help. What he had planned for today was different.

Grey tapped his request into the opaque screen set into the wall and waited as the machine beeped and loaded. It had been difficult to get a hold of the file. It was hidden behind some bureaucratic red tape by virtue of being a technical medical record and the property of MerryCom. He'd had to plead his case to one of the administration bots, explaining that it couldn't possibly be a violation of privacy to release a psych scan to the subject of that scan. The admin bot wasn't happy about it, but it capitulated in the end.

The screen flashed green: a line of script reading 'Simulation Ready'. Grey hesitated and wiped his palms on his thighs. His hands felt clammy and shaky now that he was confronted with the reality of what he was about to do. Grey took a deep breath and spun the disk to start the simulation.

The room shimmered and shifted around him, reforming into a blank white space with two chairs. Grey took a deep breath and lowered himself into one of them, his eyes locked on the other person in the room. He barely recognised himself in the man across from him. He looked younger and crueller somehow. Still, the simulation was spot on. The effect was absolutely uncanny. Grey was sitting opposite himself. The version of himself reconstructed from the medical and psychological scan MerryCom had taken right after his reanimation.

Past Grey regarded him with suspicion, his brow furrowing as his fingers clenched around the armrests of his chair.

"What's going on?" he said. "Why do you look like me?"

Grey startled hearing his own voice come from Past Grey's mouth. "I am you," he said once he recovered. "Or, rather, you are me."

Past Grey's eyes narrowed even further. "Is there a difference between us?"

"Maybe not," said Grey.

Past Grey seemed to accept that. He relaxed back into his chair and regarded Grey with cool eyes. "Why am I here?"

"I need your opinion, or…well, my opinion, I guess," said Grey. "I have questions that I can't answer on my own."

"Which are?" Past Grey raised one eyebrow and laced his fingers together in his lap, the picture of arrogant confidence. Grey studied him for a moment, recognising himself in the posture, allowing it to conjure up memories of feeling remote and unshakeable.

"Well, I guess- what motivates you?" he asked.

Past Grey smirked. "What motivates me?" his voice salivated with disdain. "What kind of a question is that?"

"It's turning out to be a rather important one," said Grey.

Past Grey looked sceptical, but Grey could tell he was considering his answer. Finally, he shifted in his seat and met Grey's gaze. "I'll only answer your questions if you answer mine."

Grey smiled. "Deal. You go first."

"I'm motivated by ambition," said Past Grey. "I want to prove my worth to the world through what I can achieve."

Grey laced his own fingers in his lap, pleased with Past Grey's candour and unsurprised by his answer. Grey suspected as much when he mulled over his Proto life. It was strange looking at Past Grey and noting the minute differences between them. Past Grey's face was clean of the stress lines around his mouth and eyes that greeted Grey in the mirror every morning. He held himself stiffly in the chair, performatively, as if warding off scrutiny with his every movement. New Grey's posture felt sloppy by comparison.

"I'm ready for your question," said Grey.

"If you and I are one and the same, I'm guessing that you're from my future," Past Grey smirked at him, though Grey could sense a desperation beneath. "Are we successful?"

Maybe he was better at reading past Grey because he remembered what it felt like to be him, remembered the exhaustion of maintaining appearances. Even now, faced with a discussion with himself, Past Grey was playing a part.

"I'm not sure how to answer that," Grey frowned. "What would you consider successful?"

A muscle twitched in Past Grey's jaw. "We must have money. Otherwise, I'm assuming you couldn't afford the technology to be having this conversation."

"We are wealthy, yes," said Grey.

"How wealthy?" asked Past Grey, only the whitening of his knuckles betraying his interest in the answer.

"Very," said Grey.

"Are we powerful?" asked Past Grey.

Grey tilted his head, considering himself carefully. "Do you want power, or control?"

"Is there a difference?" asked Past Grey.

"*I* think so," said Grey. "I think we made a lot of choices out of fear of the unknown. We sought affluence to make us feel safe."

"Maybe," admitted Past Grey. He looked unbearably sad for a moment before schooling his features back into a smooth mask. "Maybe what you call fear I call ambition."

"Maybe what you call success I call distraction," said Grey.

Past Grey rolled his eyes. "If you say so. What do you consider success, then?"

Grey chewed on the inside of his cheek, formulating his answer. "I'm not sure what success looks like for me anymore. But I know that I have everything you ever dreamed of wanting and, as impressive as it is on paper, in reality it's…," he trailed off.

"It's what?" Past Grey prompted.

"Hollow," said Grey. The word seemed to hit Past Grey like a physical blow, and he paled. He recovered quickly, glancing down at his clasped hands to collect himself.

"I see," said Past Grey softly. "Everything I dreamed of, you say?"

Grey bit back a sigh. "Yes. We are one of the wealthiest men in this century. We own the majority share of a very important company. But even with all of that, we are still lonely."

"Lonely or bored?" asked Past Grey. "You've met your goals, congratulations. Now make new ones. Dad would have coached that those accomplishments are only steps to something better."

"There's not always a next step," said Grey. "Where could we possibly go from here?"

"Expand the company. Grow the empire. Like Dad always said-,"

"Who cares what Dad said?" Grey snapped. "What he wanted doesn't matter anymore."

"Of course it matters," said Past Grey. "We have a plan,"

"Fuck the plan," said Grey, rising from his seat. "Fuck the expectations. Dad isn't here. He's been dead for hundreds of years and he's long past caring. The only person you can live for is you, because you're all you have left. Whatever hole you're trying to fill with money and power doesn't go away once you've got them, and your dead father's approval isn't worth anything."

Past Grey blinked up at him in disbelief, his eyes following Grey as he paced the room with his frustration.

"Don't you get it?" Grey said before Past Grey could work up a response. "You can change your surroundings all you want. All you've done is change the context. Different people, different places, different jobs, different times, different lives. But those parts of you, the ugly ones that keep you up at night, they follow you. They come back. And all the money in the world can't protect you from yourself."

"But the company-," said Past Grey, his eyes wide.

Grey yelled a cry of distress; overcome with every overwhelming emotion he had been carrying with him since waking up in the Ark. The intensity frightened him as his voice echoed and bounced through the room as if a thousand other Greys screamed with him. His past self sat frozen, either immobilised by shock or a glitch in the simulation, but Grey was beyond caring. He stood and turned away from Past Grey, leaning over his chair.

Eventually Past Grey resumed. "You're unhinged, Grey. Out of control. Where did you lose your way?"

Grey was triggered, he hated himself, or at least that version of him, and he gripped the chair in front of him and swung it round to throw it at Past Grey. The chair glitched through his mimic and smashed into the wall behind him. The ghost of his bullet wound shot through him and he screamed in agony, going to pick up the chair once more to swing it again and again against the chamber walls. He screamed for the old man on the battlefield, for Mish, for himself.

Pieces of the chair littered the floor with sharp splinters of glass as the simulation flickered and froze. The screen showing the simulation controls was smashed, bleeding sparking wires onto the floor and belching smoke into the air. Grey stood still, panting as he admired his work. The rage and fear were fading into a wave of catharsis, the tension falling away in sheets leaving him feeling cleansed in some way. He glanced down at his fists, slick and red with blood where his knuckles had split. He felt the pain shooting up his wrists, acute and visceral and he let out a laugh with joy that he was alive. There was an acute beauty in hurting that was entirely new to him. He felt sharpened, every sensation complete and overwhelming. He had never felt so strong, so free.

He left the simulation chamber to retrieve his tablet from the living room. Speaking with his past self had given him all the answers he needed to make his next choice. There was work to do. He had calls to make.

The first was to Serval, who answered with the bewildered frustration that Grey would expect from anybody woken in the night. Grey didn't waste time apologising for the late hour or his rude phone etiquette but barrelled straight into his point.

"I want you to stop waking Rainies from the Ark," said Grey promptly.

"You… what?" asked Serval.

"I'm rewriting company policy," said Grey. "You're not to wake any more Rainies to use as slaves. Not until we can ensure a quality of life for them in our time."

"*Slaves?*" said Serval, his voice rising an octave with his stress. "MerryCom does not employ *slaves*. To even suggest it-,"

"I promise you don't want to argue semantics with me right now, Serval. Whilst I may not have full ownership, I have enough to keep the company in a chokehold if you don't give me what I ask. I'm a man with little to lose," scoffed Grey. "Make the announcement. We're not bringing anybody back until we can promise that the world won't punish them for the time that they come from."

It was Serval's turn to scoff. "That may never happen," he said. "We'll be storing them until the end of time."

"You let me worry about that," said Grey. "Make the announcement. And when you've finished with that I want you to call Professor Brent and tell her that we're creating an accelerated programme. I want every Rainy ready to be integrated in the next two months."

"*Two months?*" sputtered Serval.

"You'll get back to your sleep much faster if you stop repeating everything I say," said Grey.

"Really, Mr. Wright, what you're suggesting, it's simply impossible," said Serval, his voice tinged with irritation. "MerryCom needs that income stream."

"Does it, Serval? I've seen the books now. You've diversified well enough to give it a go without!" said Grey. "Just do what I ask."

He ended the call, smiling to himself when he pictured Serval pacing his home anxiously, before explaining Grey's newest whacky scheme to the board. Though he didn't linger on his amusement for long, there was still work to do.

Ashby answered the call on the first ring, her tone clipped and professional as ever.

"How can I help you, Grey?" she asked.

"I want you to liquidate my remaining assets," said Grey. "I'm wiping the debts of every Rainy at MerryCom."

Ashby was silent for so long that Grey wondered if she had hung up. Finally she cleared her throat delicately and said; "Every Rainy?"

"Yes. Every single one," said Grey. "And I want to use the rest of the cash flow to pay their carbon taxes. The ones in storage too. Society needs to consider their debt paid."

"I see," said Ashby. "That's going to cause quite the stir."

"Is there anything that can stop me from doing it?"

"No, there's not," admitted Ashby. "But that much money, that many shares, the loss of labour. MerryCom will likely go insolvent. It will surely end the company."

Grey paused, clenching and unclenching his jaw. "Possibly, but it's my decision, right?"

"It is," said Ashby.

He nodded to himself. "Good."

Grey glanced down the hall toward the still-smoking simulation room. Past Grey's words echoed in his mind; *Are we powerful?* Pride ballooned in his chest. He felt powerful. Very powerful. And finally, he was going to use that power for good.

TWENTY-ONE

"Do you hear them out there?" Serval snapped, gesturing to his wall of windows with an angry hand. Beside him, Ashby's lips were a tight white line. She stood with arms crossed, observing Serval and Grey with nonchalance. Grey couldn't tell which she disapproved of more, Serval's meltdown or the protest outside.

Outside, far below Serval's cloud-tucked office, a horde of Proto protestors were screaming their displeasure at Grey's plans for the Rainies. The demonstration started shortly after the news about Grey's debt cleanse broke and gained fervour once the planned integration was officially announced.

"We can all hear them, Serval," said Ashby, her voice clipped and collected as always.

Serval scowled, turning his back to the window and running a hand through his hair. "They're going to tear this building apart,"

"That seems unlikely," said Grey placidly.

"It does, does it?" snapped Serval. "Well, with all due respect, you have no idea what you're talking about. This half-arsed scheme of yours has done nothing but enrage the public and drown this company."

"I've made my position on the future of the company very clear," said Grey.

"That's right, you have. *You don't care,*" Serval began pacing the room, his movements jerky and stiff with anger. "Forget about those of us who can't afford not to care."

Grey sighed. He surveyed Serval over his steepled fingers. "Serval, try to see past the lost profits. We're talking about people."

"People who made a *choice*. People who signed *contracts*," said Serval.

"People who took a chance and woke up as slaves," said Grey. "It's unethical. MerryCom's entire business model is predicated on forced servitude and held together by the public's prejudice. I don't think we can call this a successful venture a moment longer."

A vein bulged in Serval's forehead. "And you think throwing Rainies into that mix is a better scenario? You can train them and polish them up as much as you want, but those people down there are never going to accept them."

Ashby nodded; the movement so slight that Grey barely caught it.

"I take it you're both in agreement on this?" asked Grey.

"As your advisor, I have to agree with Serval," said Ashby.

"And as a person?" asked Grey. "What do you think then?"

Ashby bit her lip, her eyes sliding toward the window. "I don't believe in making choices for people. Your plan is certainly half-arsed, but there's dignity in it. In giving people a choice."

Grey nodded, his mind swimming with her words. He agreed with her. There was dignity in choice. But the voices from the angry mob below were pressing against the windows with a furious, pulsing beat and Grey thought that Serval might have been right as well. The Protos were never going to accept the integration easily. Some of them may never accept it. The hate was baked in too deep. In many ways, MerryCom was a safe haven for people like Grey. Like Mark.

"In that case, let's give them a choice," said Grey.

"What could you possibly mean by that?" asked Serval. Grey could tell by the flexing of his fingers that he would very much like to wrap them around Grey's throat. Grey tried not to hold it against him. It was stressful being a CEO to a failing business.

"How much does it cost to run the Ark?" Grey asked.

The corner of Ashby's mouth curled up into a smile. "Very little. The belly of the ark is self-sufficient. It's so deep underground that it's mostly powered by the heat of the earth's core."

"Perfect," said Grey.

"Do either of you want to clue me in on the plan here?" asked Serval.

"We're going to give the Rainies a choice," said Grey. "They can reintegrate as planned, or they can re-vitrify and stay stored in the Ark until public opinion shifts, knowing that upon reanimation their debts are prepaid, within our reasonable control. Obviously, MerryCom probably won't exist to reanimate them. But it's not impossible that some future company, perhaps in some future version of society altogether, will decide to revisit the, uh, human potential housed within the Ark. Including myself and Mish."

"What if public opinion never shifts?" asked Ashby.

"Nothing is as fickle as public opinion," said Grey. He met Ashby's raised eyebrow with a soft smile. "It's something my dad used to say."

Ashby raised one eyebrow. "Smart man."

"He was that," said Grey. "And a lot of other things…"

Serval stood with his hands braced against the window, gazing down at the protest below. Grey took it as a positive sign that he wasn't pacing around like a caged animal.

"Fine," he said with a heavy sigh. "We'll give them another choice. Who's going to explain it to them?"

"I will," said Grey.

"Great," said Serval, his voice dry. He turned away from the protest and levelled his gaze on Grey, crossing his arms over his chest. "That's just great. When should I tell them to prepare your pod? Before or after I tell everybody they've lost their jobs?"

Grey smiled back without much humour. "Believe it or not, Serval, I think I'm going to miss you."

*

"You're saying there are no guarantees?" asked Troy from his seat in the front of the room.

"Yes. That's what I'm saying," said Grey.

A murmur moved throughout the room as the Rainies broke into conversation amongst themselves. Grey glanced over at Professor Amy, seated beside him at the front of the room. Her mouth twisted into what Grey could only assume to be a smile, though there was little warmth to it. Grey had to beg for time at the end of her class to explain his proposition, which she begrudgingly allowed under the condition she finished her lesson in time. Grey smiled back at her. She wasn't fooling him. Class ended twenty minutes ago; she was sticking around to help talk the Rainies through a difficult decision.

Mark leaned against the wall to his right, his hands stuffed in his pockets as he surveyed the room casually. The ashen fabric of his uniform brought out the sallowness of his skin. He met Grey's gaze and shrugged, seemingly as shell-shocked by the choice as the rest of them.

Grey sighed. The insecure controlling part left deep within him ached to speak, to dispense unwarranted advice, and influence the choices made in the room. But that wasn't his job anymore. It was never his job. This was a moment for someone like Mish. She would facilitate conversation, support without suffocating, and in that moment, Grey missed her with a keenness that took the breath out of him.

"I can't tell you what to choose," he said, his voice carrying over the hushed debates. The Rainies were conditioned to speak softly. They never knew when a guard would decide to take their bad day out on them. Grey's authoritative voice was enough to bring the room back to silence. "No one can. It's a decision you'll have to make for yourselves."

"It's a gift," said Troy.

"Only if they decide to thaw us in the end," said a woman Grey recognised from the canteen buffet line. "It's not much of a gift if we're stuck as ice lollies."

"Of course there's no way of knowing if we'll have another chance at reanimation. But it's a *choice*," Grey interrupted. "It's just a choice."

"I've been outside a few times," said Matthias. He'd been sitting so quietly in the corner that Grey hadn't noticed him at first. His elbows rested on his knees and he looked down at his hands, clasped together in front of him. "The public is against us. They're turning against reanimation completely."

"Oh great," said the woman from the canteen. "Ice lolly city."

"Better than throwing ourselves to that mob out there," said Troy. "They'll tear us to pieces."

"If everyone will listen for a moment," said Amy, her reedy voice cutting through the conversation like a knife. "You'll remember from our studies; progress is often met with backlash and the screaming of the objector is often louder than the talking of the supporter. I suspect you'll find more allies than you think."

The room was quiet as the Rainies considered her words. Grey hoped she was right. It was hard to imagine allies when his ears were full of the hateful chants of the people protesting his own existence.

"I'm staying here." said Matthias in his soft deep voice. "I'll take my chances in the world I have some understanding of. Who knows what the hell the future looks like? It could be worse! Anybody who wants to stay is welcome to come with me. Safety in numbers,"

The woman from the canteen nodded at him, along with a handful of other Rainies that Grey didn't recognise. Grey smiled at Matthias, happy that a semblance of the community they had worked so hard to build was going to persist.

"I'm re-vitrifying," said Troy. "I admire those of you who are staying, truly. It's brave of you. But I'm holding out for a happier time."

The group nodding along with Troy was larger. Grey couldn't blame them. It was, after all, what he was hoping for himself.

"But what if they never unfreeze us?" asked a voice. Grey couldn't see who had spoken, but there was a murmur of voices that told Grey the question was on everybody's mind. He could feel the prickle of dozens of eyes on him.

"Again, I understand it's difficult." he said cautiously. He wished for Mish again. She would know exactly what to say.

"I heard that the mob out there might try to destroy the Ark. Doesn't that scare you?" asked another voice in the crowd.

Grey stared at his hands, white where they were braced on his thighs. "No," he said.

"No?" This time it was Cherry who spoke, her eyes very wide in her pretty face.

"No," Grey said again. "They're people. Just like us. I have to trust human nature. I'm trusting that humans know when to stop. In the pods, we're just like a graveyard to them."

Warmth blossomed in his chest as he spoke, and he knew his words were true. Night after night he went over his choices, asked himself what would happen if they never thawed him. What if they did and the re-animation didn't work? But there was no use worrying about that anymore. He was going to believe in humanity. He had to. For Mish.

"So, you're going to re-vitrify, then?" asked the woman from the canteen.

"I am," he confirmed. "I've got somebody I'm waiting to see."

*

In the end it seemed right that Mark should escort Grey back down underground into the depths of the Ark and onto his third life. It had been Mark who had introduced him to his second one, after all. But first, one last evening walk.

They strolled across the MerryCom compound, through the gardens thick with the bushes and flowers, many planted by their own hands, into the tangle of offices and hallways that made up the main building, across the breezeway, pausing to smell the mist lingering in the night air.

"Are you sure you want to give all of this up?" asked Mark as they stared out at the full moon risen round and heavy over the sleepy valley below.

"I am," said Grey, his voice thick with conviction. "It's not real without her."

Mark nodded, his throat bobbing as he swallowed some heavy emotion. Avoiding Grey's eyes, Mark reached out and clasped his shoulder. Grey was grateful for the gentle pressure tying him to the present. It would be too easy to lose himself in his thoughts and miss the way the gentle breeze stirred through the treetops and made the leaves sing. As secure as he was in his decision, it seemed important to cherish this last secret moment with a friend.

"What about you?" asked Grey. "Are you and Cherry teaming up with Matthias? Going to go carve out a place in the world for the Rainies?"

"You just want me to do the hard work so you'll have something good to wake up to," said Mark with a stiff laugh.

"Well, yeah," said Grey. "You know I'm not interested in hard work."

Mark shook his head with a smile. "At least you're honest."

"You sound like Serval," said Grey. "Only, he hates when I'm honest."

"Oh yeah?"

"Absolutely. My honesty has a nasty habit of bankrupting his company," Grey shrugged.

Mark shrugged, his smile wicked in the moonlight. "Whoops."

They stood in companionable silence for a while, nothing but the roar of the waterfall between them.

"To answer your question, I'm not sure where Cherry is going," said Mark after a while. "We split up."

"Oh yeah?" asked Grey.

"Yeah," said Mark. "Kind of had to, once she decided to stay, and I realised that I have to re-vitrify."

Grey paused, a strange sort of hopeful bubble rising in his chest. "You're re-vitrifying?"

Mark took in a deep breath and let it out with a satisfied sigh. "I am. I can't just unleash you and Mish on the future world. Who knows what trouble you'll get into without me?"

Grey studied his friend's profile as he stared out into the night. He fought the smile that was threatening to break across his features, knowing Mark would mock him for his sentimentality.

"Clearly, you are making the only responsible choice," said Grey. "Selfless of you, really."

"What can I say? I am a martyr," said Mark. He took in another deep breath and stared up at the starry sky as if he was trying to memorise it. Grey looked up as well, seized with a sudden fear that he would never see the sky like this again. That he would wake up to a future where the sky wasn't an inky black net trapping bits of light like sparkles in its void. That the valley would rot and wither without him to admire it and the waterfall would run dry leaving only a bare cliff face. He gripped the railing with his trembling hands so tightly that his knuckles went white.

"We'll be lucky to have you," said Grey softly, bracing himself for Mark's laughter.

Only the laughter never came. Mark patted Grey's back before resting his arm around his shoulder. With a heavy sigh he said, "Shall we get this show on the road?"

They walked the rest of the way down to the Ark in silence. Both lost in thoughts neither of them had the words to express. Grey thought that it was very different, facing vitrification head-on. Maybe it was easier when a bus made the choice for you. But underneath the fear, much stronger than the fear, was the anticipation—the longing for the adventure ahead and the hope that he wouldn't face it alone.

The Ark was less busy at night than it had been during the day when droves of Rainies made appointments to re-vitrify. The lobby was all but empty when Grey and Mark entered the building. The woman behind the front desk took their information and directed them to a large room down the hall where they waited until it was their turn.

"Mark?" a woman in one of the plastic suits that Grey remembered from his reanimation poked her head into the room.

"That's me," he said, rising from his seat with a wave. He glanced down at Grey and offered his hand, which Grey shook. "I'll see you on the other side then."

"See you on the other side," said Grey. He watched Mark as he left the room, his heart pounding in his throat. He was alone. And he knew that he was always going to face it alone, but the reality of the empty waiting room was intense. Luckily, he didn't have to wait for long.

"Graham?" said a man wearing the same plastic suit. "Are you ready?"

"Please, call me Grey," he said. "And I am," he rose from his seat and followed the scientist out of the room.

"The process is completely painless," said the scientist as he led Grey down a long hallway. "Like falling asleep. You won't even know what's happening. Just, blink, and you'll wake up sometime far in the future."

"Can we make a stop first?" asked Grey. "I just need to check something."

"Of course," said the scientist. "Wherever you need to go."

"Will you take me to this pod?" Grey asked, showing the number on his tablet. The scientist nodded and turned down a different hallway.

Grey followed him down a flight of stairs and into the freezing pod storage room. They wandered past rows and rows of pods before they reached Mish's. Though shaped the same, hers was larger than the others, resting on a raised platform near the centre of the room. Grey felt a surge of excitement at seeing it along with a rush of something close to homesickness. The scientist hung back as he approached the pod, seeming to understand Grey's need for a moment of privacy.

The pod was smooth and cold under his fingertips. He ran a hand across the top where he imagined Mish's head to be resting underneath. Gently, as if it was her cheekbone under his palm instead of cold metal.

"Hey, my love," he breathed. "I'm coming soon."

There was an empty pod nearby, the second prototype intended for him. Grey dragged it closer to Mish's, right next to the platform.

"This is my one?" he asked the scientist.

"Of course," said the scientist, nodding reassuringly. Grey felt a wave of peace wash over him. He wouldn't be alone, not with Mish resting beside him. They would rest together, almost like sleeping. Blink and he'd wake up with her once again in a far distant future.

"Thank you," he said to the scientist. To Mish's pod he said, "See you," and ran his hand across it one more time.

It was quiet once Grey had laid down in the vitrification chamber. The only sounds were the rustling of the plastic suit as the scientist hooked him up to various monitors and machines. Rather than making him nervous, the silence was almost reverential. There was a sense of tranquillity in the room even as the machinery started beeping, as if he was getting into bed with Mish.

"You're all set," said another one of the suits. She pressed a small round device with a red button into his hand. "When you're ready, you'll press the button. It will put you to sleep and start the vitrification process. By pressing the button you consent to being vitrified. Do you understand?"

"I do," said Grey calmly.

"Excellent. Do you have any questions before we go?" she asked.

"No," said Grey. "I'm ready."

The suit smiled at him, squeezing his hand reassuringly before motioning for the others to clear out. The door slid shut behind them with a definitive *click*. Grey ran his thumb over the button, memorising its weight and ridges. He counted his breaths - one, two, three - and pressed it. It was time.

He could smell lavender and lemons once more as the room softened and blurred around the edges. There was a press of cold, as if a chill air was solidifying around him, colder and colder and darker than anything had ever been before and then silence. Someplace peaceful and quiet. Sinking deeper and deeper and then-

Light.

*

Warm golden light pressing against his eyelids. A warmth spreading through his chest, down his arms and legs, into his fingers and toes, like sinking into a hot bath. His body relaxed like a soft sigh in a quiet room. He blinked, his eyes fluttering open to take in more of that blissful light that echoed the lightness in his limbs. Fingers flexing and arms lifting until he could see his hands in front of his eyes, the familiar scars and freckles greeting him like old friends. And then a voice, foreign and achingly familiar all at once:

"Wake up, Grey. You're home."

Printed in Great Britain
by Amazon